# THE TALES OF HORROR

[A Flip-Book]

*by Laura Mullen*

KELSEY ST. PRESS

Thanks to the editors of the following journals where portions of this work first appeared: *The Corpse, The Denver Quarterly,* and *Pataphysics* (as well as *nice-matin* & *Paris Match*).

*This voyage out in the Master's craft began with a Fellowship from the National Endowment for the Arts and two residencies at la Fondation Karolyi, Vence, France. My gratitude to Zenka Bartek (in memory) and Judith Karolyi who made the time in France possible; to Robert Antoni, Daniel Baird, Rikki Ducornet, Claudia Keelan, Nevin Mercede, Drew O'Brien, Herman Rapaport, Eddie Silva, and Dewey & Katherine Thompson: sometimes all my faith; to Carole Maso and Carol Snow: brilliant stars always with me, and Patricia Dienstfrey: the lighthouse, finally.*

Library of Congress Cataloging-in-Publication Data
Mullen, Laura, 1958–
    The tales of horror : a flip-book / by Laura Mullen
      p.   cm.
    ISBN 0-932716-48-2 (soft cover : alk. paper)
    1. Horror tales, American.  2. Plot-your-own stories.  I. Title.
  PS3563.U3955T35  1999
  813'.54—dc21                       99-29444
                                    CIP

Cover image: Paul Klee, *Zerstörter Ort 1920/215,* Inv. No. G 15638
Städtische Galerie im Lenbachhaus, Munich

Design by Poulson/Gluck Design
Text set in New Baskerville
Printed by West Coast Print Center

Kelsey St. Press    50 Northgate Ave, Berkeley, California 94708
phone 510-845-2260    fax 510-548-9185    email: kelseyst@sirius.com
web site: www.kelseyst.com

Distributed by:    Small Press Distribution    800-869-7553    email: orders@spdbooks.org

**NATIONAL ENDOWMENT FOR THE ARTS**    Publication of this book was made possible in part by grants from the National Endowment for the Arts and the California Arts Council.

*for Ruby, and Rose...*

## *The Parts:*

*Ma Pauvre Muse, hélas! qu'as-tu donc ce matin?*
*Tes yeux creux sont peuplés de visions nocturnes*
*Et je vois tour à tour réfléchis sur ton teint*
*La folie et l'horreur, froides et taciturnes.*

BAUDELAIRE

# OVERTURE

I entered the house carefully but was dismayed to find that nevertheless

*The ancient house the abandoned house the house that had been like that forever*

Despite my caution in entering in spite of the considerations I had so thoroughly

Entertained the doubts I had so prominently displayed et cetera I found that

Despite my trepidations in spite of the warnings I had received "but they were anonymous

Remember" which I had lent an ear to to which I had listened so judiciously

Which I had read and then burnt as the notes instructed but had believed

Although this had been I repeat I cannot make clear enough no sudden

Decision I did nothing in those days by fits and starts but the result of painstaking

And even I do not think I would be far off in stating exhaustive deliberations

And the weighing of all the possible consequences good and bad on both sides

The fruits of my past experiments the rather extensive if I may say so knowledge

My endless researches had finally vouchsafed me in spite of which the truth

Of the matter seemed to be that there was a point at which one could no longer say

That one was entering but that one was now in the position of 'having entered'

Although it was not certain when or if this change had occurred nor would it be possible

I quickly became aware to disentangle this having entered from what would become

a leaving

*Dark shape in its bed of rank weeds its entrance gaping but not I was wrong like that*

*Forever a shred of white lace at a broken window insisted on history*

# THE TALES OF HORROR

She touches me and takes her hand away abruptly, it's so clear that there is no one there.

"But it's always been like that!" Nervous laughter. The picture

Of a headless man falling headlong hangs at the head of the stairs.

"Why I must've been dreaming!" All this in the tone of one

Who desires to convince himself or herself. The maroon silk smoking jacket, the yawn,

The fists rubbed into the eyes. Sensuous detail is wonderful, wonderful,

But when the sheets twist themselves up into that slug-like form

In the sticky moonlight, becoming a lady who goes for the throat,

I check out of this hotel, apartment in a crumbling villa, mansion that no one…

Et cetera. "I won't stay another minute, I tell you!" Fireworks.

And if the marriage breaks up it's the fault of the house (the body

Goes out on a stretcher). "I tell you it's the same woman after all this time!"

There is a shocked gasp perhaps? Could you give us a, ah, yes—

Thought that was your tongue, no need to worry about *that* any longer.

"I say old chap, it didn't seem to you, for an instant, did it, that that *choir*

*Of summer insects* was doing Verdi?" "On the contrary…." You have to wonder

Why he didn't just donate the god-damned (whoops, literally) thing to a Museum.

He put his head in his hands. "May I make a suggestion?" "We shall have to

Arm ourselves carefully for this deed!" *And in fact he would not have lived*

*If we hadn't moved him here.* The thing, with a piercing shriek of unearthly laughter,

Fled away. "Why it's been 'to let' forever…." You can tell that a beautiful

But evil woman once lived here. Well the house was thick with terror. ("I say,

What is this goop on the stairs?") Let's have another, shall we? I don't think

I could bear to be left alone just yet. I don't think I can stay here.

These candles have a habit of going out. Ah yes, here's that little something

I've been telling you about. There, do you see that? And it's headed

In our direction. "Why, I would have sworn they…no, I'd better not have another—

Preposterous!…that those birds and insects (in the tall grasses and green-

Leaved trees at the beginning of summer) were producing a most sophisticated

Tune." Shaking his head as if to clear it. Gentle, slightly amused

Laughter, "In fact, I think I'll just turn in." Things are bound to look better

In the morning. (I believe you can shed a little light on this, Professor!)

Nothing simpler. The marks of teeth at the throat. But humming to himself

As he went back upstairs. Have you seen it? No, but I felt something, I distinctly

Felt some, as it were, breath of…. Yes, exactly: now you know I'm not mad.

I was just so grateful to find lodgings I could finally afford! As though her hand

Had frozen at the touch of my shoulder, she quickly took it—stiffened as though

Around an invisible…—away. Voices, voices, out of the walls

And the ceilings and floors. And then nothing stays where you put it.

"Why I would'na live thar sur fra hunert pound!" No Bill, nor I either—

This said kindly (condescendingly). "Tip him," this hissed out from, no doubt,

The Collective Unconscious. It had an unpromising aspect, but my funds were low,

And I wasn't, I told myself, lifting my head, one to be easily frightened.

"Just put those boxes down anywhere." And your name? *Burning eyes, eyes like….*

Ah yes, my name. I checked the mirror quickly, expecting—I'll admit it—

To find only one of us there.

❖

The curtains swayed to and fro with a ghastly drunken motion *although*

*There wasn't even a breath of....* He pressed one hand to his eyes and I saw

How haggard and pale he had recently become. "I don't expect you to believe me."

But where could I have heard this music which has been out of fashion for ages?

How had it come to lodge itself so firmly in my mind? And if I

Didn't open that window, then who...? I began to see that I was not to get answers but only

A lot more questions. The maid was incoherent with fear. Stop this gabble

And tell me what it is you've *seen.* "I can't describe it, but I felt...

With great clarity...." We tried each of the doors in turn. This house has been

Lived in, he said, speaking in a low tone but with great intensity, by an extremely

Beautiful but utterly evil woman. Yes, yes, I feel that too. This week

Workmen are taking the thing apart, stone by stone. Oh this? Just a little something

I found in the ruins. Don't bring it into the house! "It's too late," we said,

Clutching each other, and indeed it was too late. "Tell me everything you can

Recall about your mother, Mr....." They call me mad now, and say that I—

But it won't bear thinking of. And yet I must think of it, coolly,

And with the utmost logic, in order to convince you that I am not insane. "No, no,

It's impossible—and quite silly—but I'd swear to you that as I stood just now

At the head of the stairs...." "Then you saw it?" she breathlessly interrupted,

"No, but I had the clearest sensation...." "But that proves you're a (blank) too!"

And yes, I had to admit to myself, as I trudged upstairs with my small candle,

That the tainted blood of that family (I felt an absolute *frisson* of despair)

Was running in my veins as well. We must stay awake all night and watch out for it.

"Did you feel that?" "Yes." "Why, it's as though it knew we were here."

I hadn't the heart to tell her. There are things, I said gently, which you must know.

"I couldn't hope," he said, dropping his head into his hands, "you would believe me."

Then it must, I answered, in a voice almost as firm as his, be destroyed.

"Begin at the beginning and tell me everything you know about the unspeakable
Rites that were once practiced here." How well, he asked me—and I felt
That he dragged the question out of himself, reluctantly—, how well did you really
Know Mrs. (blank). My mother? I gasped, in a tone of great disbelief.
Yes, sit down, all of you—I am going to tell you something you will find
Very difficult to believe. And yet, every word of it...I swear to you.... He gazed,
For a long moment, into the fire. Yes, he said, finally, I think it is finally
Right for you to know. It was a thin piece of slightly yellowed writing paper,
Closely covered with that spidery handwriting I knew so well. "This will tell us,
I feel certain, everything we..."—this will lay your doubts to rest forever,
Oh, well, see what you think after reading this! As I read the clouds of horror
Seemed to gather ever closer about me. With what, I wondered, had I become
Involved? There was the muted sound of sobbing and yet THERE WAS NO ONE
IN THAT ROOM!
I had hoped we would have an end to this mystery before now. It's that music,
I can't get it out of my head. "No," I answered in a choked voice, "I'm afraid
That I can't believe you—not...about this." Yes, exactly the same woman—
"You can trust the evidence of your own senses I should think," he said, a crafty
Look stealing over his face. "Why yes, but I don't think they're going to
Show me any such thing as you've described." Oh, I don't ask you, any longer,
To believe me, but when empty glasses start flying through the air!
"'She's just jealous,' he murmured delightedly, 'murderously....'" *Listen,* —
This with a hand outflung to still us —*yes, there...I just heard it again....*

❖

Yes, said the Doctor, tipping his head back to let the sweet

Burning fluid slide down his throat, I remember a similar tale,

But a tale so horrible in all of its implications....

He paused, looking out at us as though to see whether we would,

As an audience, *do*—and then turning again to the depths of his empty

Glass he continued, in a softer tone, as though he were speaking

To himself. As though there had been no time in between. "I remember

Everything." And then, looking up, his voice more insistent, "*everything*."

(At last we got it out of her. At last she murmured a few words between

Fits of hysterical weeping. At last she was able to get out a few

Broken sentences. "Oh well," he said, "if *that's* all it was!")

"It was on a night just such as this one." (All at once the rotten

Wood gave way beneath me and I was falling, falling, the echo

Of that inhuman laughter ringing in my ears.) As though there were no time

In between. The room I woke up in closely resembled, and yet...

Something was subtly...changed. And not for the better, needless

To say. "Here, take this, go get yourself something

To take the chill off." Tipping his hat, "Thankee." At last I was alone.

I breathed a huge sigh—too soon of course, though how could I

Have known—of relief. *Yess*, that voice whispered, out of the seemingly permanent

Gloom, *now it's just you and me.* Eh? Oh, I say—must've been dreaming,

And yet I could've sworn...but there it is again: that series of peculiar,

Oddly haunting noises that seem always to be on the point of arranging themselves

Into a recognizable (if unfamiliar and somewhat out-dated) *chune.*

❖

All at once, and with her eyes still closed, she rose from her chair and swayed

Gently from side to side as though to a music we could not hear. "There,"

He breathed, "what did I tell you?" And yet if you wake her now she will remember

Nothing. We must fetch the Doctor at once. But neither of us made a move

Towards the door. "Are you sure you'll be alright here, alone, tonight?"

He glanced down anxiously and then let his eyes slide past me to the stains

On the floor near the gaping entrance to the cellar. "Oh yes, I'll be fine."

"It is, of course," began the Doctor, slowly and in a tone of great sorrow,

"A love story first of all." We suspected him, by then, of being capable of any

Kind of rank sentimentality which might suit his nefarious purpose, but perhaps

He was just a bit tipsy after all. He gazed moodily into the fire. It was

A night much like this one, he began. We drew our chairs closer.

"I wish you could promise me that nothing will happen to you." "I promise,"

I smiled, with a swift look over my shoulder, "now shoo." I heard the jaunty

Sound of his cane as he followed the iron fence back out into the increasing fog.

Was it my imagination or did these noises, even as they faded, resolve themselves

Into a piece of music,—a 'little phrase,' a tune? "Yes it is," he remarked,

But still more softly (as though to convince himself), "a love story, first and last."

I shook her violently. Stop it. You'll only frighten her more.

He heard the screams beginning from two blocks away, "faster,—my God, man,

Can't you hear?" "Eer whut, guv'ner?" It was only then that I noticed

It had no face. "I'm afraid we're too late." "Yes," distractedly, feeling in vain

For her heart, "much too late." "It will be easier," he said, giving each of us the benefit

Of his piercing regard, "for most of you here tonight not to believe me."

But you, *cher Professor*, will know I am telling the truth.

❖

Dr. Silence comes onstage again,

Bows, motions as if to make

An orchestra apparent only to himself

Begin playing. "Odd how the steady dripping

Has begun to resolve itself, begins to…

Resolve itself…." "Into a dance tune

Of thirty years ago?" (A Popular Song.)

"Then you hear it too?" "I used to

Hear it everywhere—or so it seemed."

Pearls, bare shoulders, perfume…

(A Grocery List)—sensuous detail—

*Which reminds me*: "Yes, now I remember

Everything." "Ah, I'd forget my head

If I didn't have it…." Hackneyed and expensive

Sensuous detail: "she was oddly pale."

"Yes, well," he laughed gently, shuffling

The sheaf of notes I'd handed him—

"If you really *could* recall it," (I seemed

To hear that "n'est-ce pas?" coming

From a long ways away as the floor

Gave way beneath me and merciful

Blankness closed in) "you wouldn't

Have had to write it down, now would you?"

I'm sure I didn't imagine that sneer.

❖

"Ah, come in, come in—I've been expecting you." I tried hard to keep the sound of
    fear

(Mmm, yes, he said, listen,—there it is again, that very interesting cadence,

That pattern of notes with a falling…) out of my voice. The room

Grew suddenly colder. "Wait…." She looked away for a moment, but not at anything—

It was as though she were listening to something within herself—"I almost had it:

I very nearly remembered what it was." We must be perfectly quiet. I have let my terror

Run my life, but no longer. "You can set those bags down anywhere." I tried hard

To keep the rising sound of hysteria out of what I liked to think of as my voice.

"The Doctor…" I said, but it was too late: whatever it was, with its promising

Glimpses into those darker reaches of the mind, had vanished entirely.

As though, need I add, it had never been. He laughed a little self-consciously

And tossed back the last of the amber fluid, "Oh, I'd tapped into mysterious forces

All right…bloody glad to feel myself again, I can tell you!" (This last

Said nervously.) "Course you are!" *But Doctor, look at the marks it made!*

*Yes*, he said, clutching his brow and turning away from the sight—*it's happening*

*All over again.* But I felt drawn on by a power much larger than myself.

You must tell me *everything* you remember about her. Everything? Start with the last

Night you saw her alive. Yes, here are the marks, he murmured sadly,

His knuckles white as the handful of lace he pulled roughly aside,

Just as I feared—right where we expected them.

Of course, I breathed, closing my eyes, in her throat.

❖

"I think you must have been," she whispered,

"Terribly alone for a long, long time." All at once

I felt myself falling, falling into a blackness so complete

It was as though the walls and floors....

Hit her if you have to, he said drily,—we have got to know

What it is she thinks she's seen. "So alone," she went on,

In a voice so intimate I wasn't sure it wasn't

Coming from within me, "you were sick with it: you felt it

Eating you up from inside: you thought you were

Dying." Abruptly she took her hand away.

He wrote me a letter. These candles have a habit

Of going out at the oddest times. Sobbing with relief,

"Then you *believe* me?" He stood in the street

Watching the lighted windows go out, one by one.

*There is something*, he whispered into the fog, *that I think you must know.*

"A love story!" Someone in the back row gasped in disbelief.

"Yes, yes," he said, but as if to himself, "I think that is what you would

Have to call it." Then what you are saying, I murmured at last, is that none of us

Can be trusted. He looked slightly annoyed. I was coming to that.

These are not, he said shrilly, empty assertions, these are facts—

Based on experiments. Yes, she said in a low tone and as if unwillingly,

It is true that I have had some luck in causing what you might call the essence

To reappear. But then we must all, he repeated, be perfectly silent.

I deciphered the mad scrawl on the fragment of yellowing parchment with some difficulty

And a growing sense of disease. I'm afraid it may indeed be a love story.

But these words, he said, looking up from the page, mean nothing to me.

# Things Look Better in the Morning

The sense of having been mistaken in all of my,—well, what would you call them?

Fancies, I think, is the word that springs to mind, came to me strongly

As I sipped my coffee where the first pale rays of sunlight reached in

Through the narrow windows. The place just needs a few improvements, that's all.

"Sleep well, darling?" "Mmmm, yes." "Not bothered by any, heh heh, little *noises*,

Were you?" "What? Oh, oh…no, not at all. And you?" "Don't be silly."

The maid, quiet and sensible, although (mercifully, I suspected) unable to remember

Anything, shakily dished out the brains onto each of our plates. "Now I don't want to see you

Talking to the police later," my husband said, "if you remember anything, anything at all,

Come to me." She nodded weakly. "Dear," I said, when the door had closed behind her,

"You'll only frighten her more." "Maybe frighten some sense into her," he replied,

But with what I could tell was only an assumed gruffness, retreating behind the paper.

I recall, though it seems a million years ago, the light-hearted ease with which

I went about my little chores that day. Why, I might even have been singing to myself again,

After so long! But it all seemed so simple, on that bright morning: a little paint,

Some flowers, a scattering of vividly-colored silk cushions, to pick out the harmonies…

"And we'll have to get in a piano!" Even my darling (blank) no longer accused it of being

'A mad plan.' In fact he expressed an interest—for the first time—in the history

Of the old pile, and when I found him poking, with a speculative look in his eye,

At the foundations with the tip of his umbrella I considered it an excellent sign.

"You won't," I sung out a bit anxiously (for the maid's pale, questioning face

Had appeared at one of the dormer windows in what we thought of as the empty wing),

"Track any of that indoors, will you?" "No," he called back, clearly replying

To some other question, "no,—I think I'll be staying outside." He was always like that:

Amazingly sensitive. "Is it still 'feminine intuition'," he used to ask,

"When it's something *I* have?" It's an experience, the Doctor had had to explain to me,

From which he may never recover. I see it all so clearly now and I am able, yes,

To pity him. But who would have guessed, on that lovely morning, that either of us

Might soon be an object of pity? "We must," I trilled, "plant something there!" Indeed.

It is only in recollection that I can see how we were menaced, even then, by unseen

Forces, forces which would soon…that is to say, *which would all too soon….*

These moments of relative peace seem all that much more something in comparison.

"A dark substance oozed up from the holes he had made…."

And yet it was, in looking back, as though I already knew,—

Or perhaps I should say already suspected, for surely I would not have known

To grasp so desperately at, and attempt to 'treasure,' those fleeting instants

As I did without…. To all but crush in this mad desire to keep unless, somewhere,

Somehow…. "Yes, it is all too true," he said sadly, wiping off the point of his umbrella,

"One must have a profound sense of death in order to properly live."


All of us, as we left the fire-lit room, were forced to confess

That we had never heard anything so patently absurd.


❖


Although there was not a breath of wind

The candle I was holding abruptly went out.

"Yeah," I said, "my heart *is* breaking; what do you care?"

There has to be a moment like this for a moment like this in the

And I was

Plunged into the most profound what, what? There wasn't

From here a word I could get it into. "As though the walls and the floor…."

Never mind, I said, I'm used to it.

And I was used to it: the longing, the beautiful words, the thinking for a moment

I might not be alone (that I might not be alone), but the softness in her voice,

The mere music undid me, "There has to be a moment for this moment,"

She said that is not what she said, "Your heart is breaking,

Isn't it." And "Yes, my heart is breaking," I said. In the something I felt the some-

Thing touch of uh huh, uh huh. "Listen," he whispered, "that music...."

We took up the graceful attitudes that nothing can ever change. No. "Listen,"

He raised his hand, "the piano...." He made us see how we could fall subject

"To the highly persuasive feeling," and here he,

Turning back to us after 'just freshening up' his drink, allowed himself

A small, almost rueful smile, "that there is no longer a thing such as chance,

*Soi-disant* coincidence or, more clearly,

The extraneous: but that everything could become, *is* becoming

A part of this, if you will, ephemeral, tenacious

Lace being woven—(this dazzling, intricate)..." he paused,

"Net, or veil, or web—at the same time woven and," looking not at us,

But deep into the fire, "undone: everything

becoming part of this... I would have to say *music*, romantic music; everything

Playing in.... And yet I fear," he mused, glancing down once more at the ragged

Shred of foolscap, burning and falling away to ash in his hand,

"There was no one in that room."


❖


*Two Letters*

1)  Wed. 5/11/88

Dearest...

I've thought of writing you every day because I think about you often (I find myself day-dreaming about you ((blush))). Things have been hectic.... I just want to explain quickly here in this note that I was quite taken by you and was frustrated that we did not have more time to get to know each other. I didn't mean any harm by my er, proposition, and it is not my usual way of doing things but (if you think this was stupid so far, it just gets more so) I was afraid that you'd fall in love with a Frenchman (it wouldn't feel as bad losing out to any other nationality) before I, or should I say we, had a chance to get to know each other. I want to read your poems, I would like to hear you read them to me, you make me laugh—I'd like to laugh some more with you and I'm aching to embrace you, to kiss your cheeks, your neck and then to slowly press my lips against yours and have the moment linger forever. This may sound impulsive, but I'm not a kid anymore and I think I'm in touch with my feelings. I haven't seen anyone steady in awhile, dating sure, but no one has struck me as you have and you can't blame it on France either because it happened at JFK. I'll write you properly soon.

affectionately…


2)  5/15/88

Dear…

How is your writing going? I can't wait to read/hear one of your poems. I also can't wait to see you and talk to you but I suppose I'll have to wait after all. Spring is here in full force—there are some rainy days.…

    5/25

It is true that as we get older time passes much more quickly. So much has happened since I returned.… I suppose that I have procrastinated in writing to you in part because I feel awkward about several things: first of all I presume that you are a master of language usage and that I couldn't possibly impress you with language. Second I fear losing something I have not possessed yet (if possessed sounds sexist you may substitute shared). —— darling, I just want you to know that I was so taken with you so quickly that it is frightening. When I asked you to spend the night with me I did not mean to sound disrespectful to you. My emotions were so overwhelming that I could not express myself calmly or rationally, every vestige of 'suaveness' left my demeanor entirely. I did want to show one thing—that I was very attracted to you (I DO NOT make sexual advances lightly). What would not come across was how I imagined everything would take place in my mind: I imagined that we would go back to G—— together, go for a walk nearby holding hands, stop in a field and turn our faces to the heavens in silence, then look into each other's eyes and slowly our lips would be drawn to each other's, together, slowly as if by a superior, magical, irresistible force, our lips would just barely touch at first then press together ever so slowly, lingering over every innuendo of each particular of each other's lips. This first kiss would last an eternity, time would stand still and accelerate to light speed at the same time. Then we would walk back to the house light-headed and drunk with our passionate and lusty kisses.

6/1

We would then undress each other and sit in the hot tub, on opposite sides, the soles of our feet pressed together, touching in a primal way — the feet being our most primitive body part (our hands are the most evolved). Lastly we would sleep together, holding each other, perhaps our lips still lightly touching — since we would have drifted to sleep after thousands of little kisses.

Well, that's how I dreamed it would be. So I'm a romantic — I hope you are not disillusioned that I hadn't written as soon as I said I would. Events have been taking place at a very fast rate of speed. We have had some good weather and I have been to the beach a few times and it was very pleasant and relaxing. The water temperature is somewhat bracing at first exposure but otherwise quite pleasant.

I know that you are coming to N— Y— in July. I don't recall what day exactly but I feel as though I am being tortured and may not survive to see you return. I considered describing myself but am not sure of how to do it without sounding like a personal ad. I hope that I come off as a basically decent chap (aside from asking you to sleep with me on our first date — and no I didn't think you were that kind of girl. I still can't help but smile when I recall your reply "No I don't think so…," spoken a little flat, not quite toneless and your facial expression was priceless as well — a mixture of disbelief, horror, and fascination I think. I was feeling terribly shy and embarrassed all night and I don't know if I could have come across as anything but awkward and comical…) and I like to be serious as well as funny and silly. I'm a hard worker because I enjoy what I do and I see the potential for a very pleasant and comfortable future. I like to read, exercise and be outdoors as much as possible. Rent movies, go to the movies. Music — I have been buying CD's lately.…

6/2

Well, I think it would be asking for too much to try and conclude this rambling of free associations in any reasonable manner so I'll bid you au revoir. Do write if you can.

My fondest and most affectionate regards

and one thousand gentle kisses upon your face,…

*(margin note, pp 1–3)*
It just occurred to me that I've only been using up 7/8ths of these too small pieces of paper and it only makes me smile and think of Samuel Beckett and how he has dedicated his life to expounding the idea that man is a creature of habit destined to be so because he is a prisoner to the limitations of his body and its (the body's) necessary functions.

❖

" 'Connected,' but how?" I had to admit there was a part of me that hoped she would never remember. "It is clear," he said at last, "that there is at least one of you here in whose interest it is that she never remember." I glanced hastily toward the French doors. Was I that transparent? "But you must," someone sobbed, twisting uselessly in the firm grasp of the attendants, "you must let me explain." There'll be time enough for that later. He took me by the hand, "But then," fixing his stare on me all the while, "you have decided?" "Oh yes," I gushed, "I think I loved it from the first…and then the price…," smiling and rolling my eyes up, minstrel style. "Oh ho, the *price*," he giggled (impossible not to become infected by his laughter), "the merest pleasantry, really!" "Yes, yes," I gasped, "a joke!"

❖

*I had to wonder if I wasn't just trying to scare myself.*

"It's a great property value." "Could you tell me
A little bit about the place?" An odd look, sidelong.
"I mean, it looks like it's been empty for a long time."
"Well, we get a lot of people looking at it,
A lot of interest being shown, and you know
You're not going to find a better price for a house like this."
"Uhm…," running my hands across the sharp-edged,
Sere grasses in what must once have been
The front yard. "And it's got a lot of history." "Oh,"
Lifting to my mouth my 'encarmined' palm, "oh yes,
I expected that." What does it mean, *our eyes "met"*?

*Cash changed hands.*

"But it would be nice to talk to the former owners
Sometime; d'you suppose I could ask them to call on me?"
He crossed himself quickly, muttered, "And pray
To the good Lord they had a prior engagement."
"What's that?" "Well, they're every single one of 'em
Dead." "Oh yes, well…I see what you mean," I said.

*We bored holes through each other with our eyes.*

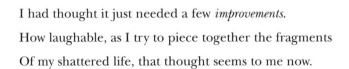

I had thought it just needed a few *improvements.*
How laughable, as I try to piece together the fragments
Of my shattered life, that thought seems to me now.

# (BELATED) PROLOGUE

*"J'ai le droit de faire ce que je veux avec mon corps!"*

(CHER)

But there didn't exactly seem to be a beginning.

I glanced down at the (torn and yellowed)

Scrap of paper in my hands—

The manuscript my somewhat over-zealous cleaning-woman

Had found behind the…

Which the author's trusted friend had refused to…

Which had lain forgotten until now in the…

Which could be released to the public only now

On the death of (blank)

On whom the author so clearly had based the main character…

Discovered mouldering in the—oh yes, I like that:

"Discovered mouldering,…its singed edges…"—

*Oh yes*, he murmured, *I like a woman with a past!*

"A beautiful, but," and here he paused significantly,

"I cannot stress this point enough,

Thoroughly evil woman once inhabited this house."

There was a horrified gasp. Would the scent

Of her perfume still lingering on the air be too much?

No? "My Sin," of course.

❖

We began to feel that there was some point at which the truth might be important—the

bare truth, that is: the *facts* of the matter—but whether in fact that point had been

reached (or even, but it hardly bore thinking of, passed entirely), this we could not, with

any certainty, say. "But I felt, distinctly.…" How…odd,—well, all of the windows are shut,

aren't they? And yet, just here, there is a terribly chill draft, which cuts, as they say, to

the bone. And where is that strange blue light coming from? (A desire to run the movie backwards up to a certain point and then say, and then see oneself saying, firmly, *this* time, "get out of my bed," —a useless desire....) Well, if it would make you feel better, she said, you could always take the test. Ah, yes, and then—having the slate wiped clean, you see (having the proof of it: nothing happened, because that was the assumption, wasn't it—nothing had...), *start*—but you could see this coming a long ways away, couldn't you—*over*. Ah yes, start over again, none of it having mattered, or not very much. But it isn't that simple; it isn't quite that simple.... But it has captured my imagination: the idea of starting over again, *clean*.

❖

*Long shreds of cobwebs clinging, wrapped themselves around her ever more thickly as she ran— but cautiously, testing each step on those weak, those rotting floorboards—toward your voice through the succession of empty, echoing rooms, until she was entirely enmeshed, covered, so that, when you saw her—reflected dimly in what was left of the silvered surfaces in the famous 'hall of mirrors,' veiled in and trailing some echo of their tarnish—what you saw there sent you running too, and screaming....*

❖

He said he would have to build this woman up out of...fragments; or no, that's what he said later, much later, what I think he might have said then was this, was something like this: that it was only in pieces, or 'piecemeal,' that we could hope to come to understand her: that we would have to break her down, as it were, in order to build her up, "out of these...." He insisted we look at each part separately, so as to better grasp the whole; the, "if you will, *gestalt.*" "Remember that we are not the first," he smiled, "to insist on such an accounting; though no one, before this, has probably ever taken it far enough." You will want to make lists, he said, you will want to keep detailed records, catalogues, files, inventories. Don't worry, he told us then, laughing, putting her back together again is the easy part.

❖

## Cher: Les Secrets de sa Magie
*DIX RETOUCHES POUR UNE SILHOUETTE DE LEGENDE*

**VISAGE:** en 1981, elle débourse 12 000 F pour effacer des traces d'acné.

**NEZ:** Cher, qui le trouvait "gigantesque", se décide à le faire rapetisser en 1987 pour 24 000 F.

**MENTON:** en 1987, elle se fait injecter de la silicone pour en parfaire la forme. Elle en profite, moyennant 18 000 F, pour rendre ses pomettes plus saillantes grâce à un implant de matière plastique et pour faire "arranger" ses dents.

**SEINS** (1re opération): lasse de voir ses tailleurs "tomber comme des sacs", elle fait remodeler sa poitrine dès 1969, pour 30 000 F.
**SEINS** (2re opération): mécontente de ses seins devenus "flasques" après de la naissance de son fils, elle les fait remonter, en 1979, pour 30 000 F.
**SEINS** (3re opération): en 1983 elle dépense de nouveau 30 000 F pour donner à sa poitrine le galbe qu'elle estime idéal.

**CÔTES:** afin d'amincir sa silhouette et d'avoir "l'air d'un garçon", elle se fait enlever en 1980 deux côtes inférieures.

**FESSES:** la diva, au début des années 80, se serait fait prélever un peu de la peau des cuisses pour en corriger l'arrondi. Il lui en aurait coûté plus de 30 000 F.

**NOMBRIL:** elle a oublié à quelle date elle en a fait, pour 18 000 F, réduire le diamètre tout en se faisant retendre la peau du ventre.

**CUISSES:** elle perd en 1980 cinq centimètres de tour de cuisses et, pour 24 000 F, s'en fait également tirer la peau.

❖

"We are speaking," he said, gazing into the fire as though it held some vision,

As though events were being enacted within it which only he could see,

As though he were reading from a book which he alone…, "of property values,"

Which he alone of all of us was privileged to find there, I finished, lamely;

A book in a language lost, he said, in any attempt at…—

*"Real,"* he added, turning his speculative gaze upon us each, *"estate."*


❖


"I must begin," he repeated, lifting his empty glass to the firelight as though he were

gazing—back at those far distant events—through it (or, as mine host could not help

thinking, as though to call attention to its emptiness), "at the beginning." In the breath-

less hush which followed these words we could all distinguish the eerily rhythmic scratch-

ing of the apple tree's bare branches against the tall windows. "It was on a night almost

exactly such as this one…"; or, "It was during the war, of course, but even for those trou-

bled days it was an unbelievable price." Why I feel, I remember saying to the agent—a

hachet-faced man with a gash of a smile and a grip of iron and silk—as though I were

*stealing* it from you! I wouldn't, he answered, throwing back his head as if to give free rein

to his laughter, feel that way at all if I were you. Dammit,—I was tempted to hit her, to

throw a glass of cold water in her face. "It's no use," the Doctor said, rising, "she may not

be able to tell us what she saw," he looked at each of us in turn, "ever." I could see it was

time to face facts.

❖

Something like, *"The throat so horribly slashed I believed for an instant the head was detached from the trunk,"*—but that's only a rough translation.

❖

Muffled by fog ("deadened"), I heard the bell at nearby St. Something's
Tolling the hour. "It won't be long now," he said.
"Well it's a consistent ghost at least," I laughed, a little unsteadily.
"Oh yes," he said, but as if to himself, "it is
My most regular visitor." *I am not sure*, the Doctor announced,
*That he will ever*, after what happened, after the events that took place here, after
Witnessing all that he did, after the terrible shock his system has received,
*Be the same*. "Am I losing my mind?" I asked,
As the glowing cloud rose ever higher into the clear dawn air,
"Am I losing my...." "There," he said, "there it is again!
Listen!" Yes, faintly but distinctly, from the side of the house we knew to be empty,
The fragile beginnings of what I could only believe to be a...
(Replete as it was with certain repetitions).
"Doctor," I said, as he pulled the door of the sickroom shut behind him,
"You must tell me everything,—there is no need to break it to me
Gently—you must be completely honest (if it is not
Already too late); I have," I said, more firmly than I felt, "a right to know."
He put a fatherly hand somewhere. "You will be pleased when I tell you,"
He told me, "as I am able to tell you, in good conscience, that he
Is dying of the disease, quite clearly: not the cure." And I was pleased;
Indeed, I think it is safe to say we all were. Okay, *we all were.*

Invisible hands moved among the tea things. The book I left lying open

Was riffled through quickly and snapped shut. The curtains

Swayed drunkenly although there was not a breath

Of wind in the house. "Isn't anyone," I shouted despairingly,

My voice lost in those vast reaches so recently claimed

For mankind, "responsible?!" The Doctor made a soothing motion,—

"I believe," he said, and the conviction in his voice could not fail

To impress me, "that there must be some human agent,

Causing, through great force of will, all of these seemingly inexplicable

Events to take place." "But then we must," I said, rising, as good as my word,

"Destroy it immediately!" "You have not understood me," he pouted.

With a faraway look in his eyes he looked far away.

"This 'agent,'" he wrote, "may be very far away."

# The Tales of Horror

*There have been times when I was not sure,* I read,

*I would have the strength to tell you…—or that you could bear….*

I felt as though the floor—it was suddenly as though the floor

Had given way beneath me, as though I were falling through a darkness without

Weight or substance, simply drifting, "falling and drifting…," the sound of my screams

Seeming to come from a long way off. But, *There are things*

*Which I think you must know.* I glanced down at the scrap of singed and yellowed

("Folded, spindled…" et cetera) paper I held in my grasp. Already those few words

Were fading from memory. "She has had," he asserted, snapping-to the clasp

Of his little black bag, "a terrible shock." He was never averse to a little hard cash.

As if of its own volition his apparently unconnected outstretched hand….

"Thank you," I said, looking down on that slumped and finally quiet form.

"The pleasure was mine," he answered (meaningfully?).

"But I cannot go on with my story," he cried, startling us all from our reverie,

From the spell he had woven, from the far distant places his tale had led us to,—

"You must be tired," this added more gently, "and it is, I fear, very late."

But we implored him to take up, again, the thread of his narrative. "Why I don't

believe,"

Someone in the back piped up, "I could sleep a wink!" A pleased smile, "Well,

If you feel that way about it, of course, I can and will continue…."


❖


Was it a dream, as he insisted, patched together from these fragments of memory? He has

constructed, the Doctor said carefully, an entire world which revolves around the idea he

has —in your absence—developed of you. Had there ever really been a woman in a long

white dress pirouetting through those empty rooms, "forever," skirt slowly blackening where it brushed through the soot that blanketed what remained of floors and walls? "It's all yours," he said. It was all mine now. Our eyes had met and locked; I felt my breath catch in my throat and heard what I thought must be my heart, beating. I signed the papers. Cash changed hands. There was a good explanation, he said, for every single one of these sounds. Scattered bits of broken glass, when the sun came suddenly out, glittered dangerously. Don't come any closer. But was it a white lace veil lifted up by the force of her dancing, or only a drift of dank fog through those ruins which winter held still?

❖

"None of my usual remedies, I'm afraid," he said gently,
"Are going to do us any good." Are going to be of any use
To us here today. "Do you understand," he asked harshly,
His voice cracked, his parched lips bleeding as he spoke,
"'La gorge si horriblement tailladée, que j'ai cru
Un instant....'" "Shush, darling,—you shouldn't try to speak yet."
Too late, too late,—I felt the words (loud as they seemed
In my head) must be audible to everyone. I knelt
To wrap that figure where it lay in the sun-faded
Square of expensive silk he had favored, covered
With elegant sketches of insignia and details from the uniform
Of an Austrian soldier. His lips were still moving, his eyes wildly
Rolling around the room. "Understand...," he muttered again,
And then, beckoning us closer, a pleased, idiotic smile
On his face and his features
Finally at rest, he remarked—softly (as though it were

To remain somehow a mystery, even as he explained it) —

That a beautiful but, "utterly, utterly…evil

Woman…." I envied him his experience of that: his pure experience.

Don't try to speak now, darling. He shut his eyes

Against the sudden light; as if against the; or as though to, —

But there wasn't. *I can feel you thinking*, she sighed.

❖

*There were holes where something large had attempted to eat its way in.*

❖

"Do not," this whispered low, little more than a breath

Between those dry lips as they lifted him onto the stretcher,

"Do not forgive her." What was it inside me that knew

It was the only time I would ever hear him speak of the strange

Events which had befallen him in that terrible house which seemed—

now, in the innocent light of day—to be so utterly at peace: empty

Even of its disturbing associations. (Or any plausible explanation

Of how I found myself here, playing 'the dumb blond,' "Who, me?"

*Dans cette nuit américaine*, to reassure him, "Why, I'd forget my head if….")

"No," I said savagely, into the silence (for the sound of those screams

Had died out long ago), "I never will." But it would be years

Before I came to understand the meaning of that vow.

❖

*("It's falling apart all around us," I said, "can't you tell?")*

❖

The sound of what was or could have been I couldn't tell

A "little phrase" but played this time on a more delicate instrument

Rose up out of the darkness alone a sobbing held

I thought a broken

Sobbing held pulled taut and plucked upon

As if there were

A secret sorrow in this house which could be

Wrested out. "Make her drink this."
Here, drink this—it will make you feel

Better. But I couldn't force the fragile edge
Of that too-long-held and too-much-drawn-out

Note between her chattering teeth. "Throw the contents
In her face then, if you have to." I looked back at him

In horror. "I can always make another," he said casually.
I knew then that he did not see as I did:

That when we stood together looking out on the green
Fields which stretched away on every side

Of the estate he was seeing through them
To the gaping holes, sometimes miles wide,

Out of which he would claw what he had come to think of
As *a living.* "Don't you understand," I said to him,

But it was far too late, "you cannot make me
Any safer than I am."

*"It was on a night like this one...."—*
*Raised eyebrows, open mouths, a look*
*At least of disbelief from his audience...—*
*Could there ever have been*
*"'A night like this'"?*

Noises you couldn't trace from the walls and ceilings and floors, slight at first, but growing louder, getting closer, until you begin to think you are going out of your mind.
I started violently from my chair. But there was no reflection in the mirror, no hand
hefting that empty glass suddenly into the air, no one to come home to. "It is a story," he
said (or was it "an old story"?), "that takes a long time to tell." There was a draft although

none of the doors or windows were open. He rotted away in an instant as we watched. *The head was almost detached from the body.* The writing faded in my hand. I am sure that she knows more—a desperate look in his eyes—than she is telling us. Do you think you will have to operate? "Set the bags," I said, lightly (trying to keep the terror out of my voice), "down any old where." *Here,* he said, *drink this.* "I feel," I said, "I feel so…," but I could never find the words.

# A Travel Diary

*(As if I'd been caught with the sheet draped over me:*
*The all-too-explicable cause of these sounds,—of these*
*"Disturbances." I clanked the chains and moaned.)*

❖

I had begun to feel I had to find a beginning or

To "find my way back to a beginning," not,

Of course, *la même chose.* "But *none* of these people,"

She sobbed, brokenly,

"Seem at all real to me." I picked them up, one by one,

And gave them a good shaking.

"We'll get that ticker working again in no time."

Thinking, not saying, *I hope not.* There—

That proves it:

You do have a 'mysterious inner life.'

❖

But THERE WAS NO ONE IN THAT ROOM. Voices

Out of the walls and ceilings and floors.

He leaned closer, "Now, you seem like the kind of girl…"—

Or was it, "exactly the kind of girl"?—

"To take," gesturing

Vaguely behind him toward the burning

House in its crown of flames, its veil

Of smoke, "Home…." I held

My breath,

Waiting for him to go on….

❖

GARE DE L'HORREUR

*"A la suite, semble-t-il, d'une erreur ou d'un mauvaise fonctionnement d'aiguillage, un*
*train…entrant à vive allure…a broyé…en début de soirée…."*
(As, shaken
But unhurt, you brush the shattered
Glass from your skin.) (You,
*Hypocrite…*et cetera.)

❖

*As the train pulls away as the view or landscape or prospect is snatched backward as the given-*
*out is taken away as outside the window the oily flow of the other tracks which are always the*
*same something is wrong here beside which and beginning now to blur so each tree is a twitch*
*in the green which is all that stays true long enough for me to as we say get it down the distinc-*
*tions are slipping away is this a beginning (again clean) the once-upon-a-time storybook land-*
*scape (flicker of house cow darker green meaning forest snap of flame at a transient camp where*
*the ramshackle) vomited by or so it seemed to this viewpoint I am being violently hauled away*

❖

"Since he got the third test back," she said drily, "with the results still negative,
He's stopped talking about dying. To continue to do so would be embarrassing."

It means an end

No doubt, to finding him—as we did last spring—looking for the tell-tale "purple spots," in a cafe, his pants hiked up above his knees.

(This is perhaps the scene you were thinking of?)

*"S'etait replongée dans l'onde opaque...."*

❖

(What is/was outside)
The Window

A skylight in a cage
Set into a roof of tin. A sign,
"Marché de la Gare."
Wet streets and the shine
Of the other rails beside which become
*Shine*—this strip of reflected
Green which flickers against a grey
Light. The occasional
Poppy: a red (gone)
Against the blur of various
Greens. Walls. Backs
Of houses; hung out to dry the white
Sheets, the gaily patterned
Skirts and blouses. Rusted parts
Of machines. These—
In a sudden clearing—
Small black birds flung wide
Above a field of green-gold wheat.

Framed in a window the glimpse of a lifted
Hand and a face.

❖

(And the vision which lifts these shapes
Up out of the shifting, possible, anything,
Pulls—and distorts—from this flux a still
Figure, a gesture.)

*"Un instant...détachée...."*

❖

Hurled, it seemed, through the silvered leaves,
The turning leaves of the poplars outside
The Hôtel Biron, lifted and turned by the storm and the silver
Knife-flash of sunlight, swiftly; it was raining
Off and on: the shadows lifted
And set down by this
Light from between clouds; solidity itself
(It seemed) lifted and set down: these human
Shapes pulled up out of (intermittently)
The whiteness,
The unformed....

But twisted, distorted to display
These finished
Surfaces—the "beautiful"—
To the gaze....

Which makes of everything seen,
Seized, a detail
Of the *"Portes d'Enfer."*

❖

The scent of fresh melon fills this section
Of the train, "of freshly cut"
(Deeper in), *Honeydew*

(Which is not
The word for it here).

❖

Here it is all in reverse: we look through flesh to find the squirm of bloody muscle caged in bone, "the heart of the matter," pumping in and out in its obscene…squeeze, as though the truth were there to get ahold of, finally, get a grasp upon, to seize…release and seize. I lifted up the gold-flecked, blue-gray, gun-metal skin of the trout on my plate. "The splendidly furnished rooms," we need to see through, here, to ruin ("but it is death which keeps," he kept insisting, "this love alive…"), wishing time upon, reminding us our days are *short, few, numbered*; that we are "dying, Egypt, dying": that we do not have long. He said, again, that he did not have much time. I reached for the cream, smiled, changed the subject—'on to brighter things.' *I know you will die*—should I have said that? And added, "this latest illness terrified me"? Now he is putting to good use what he well knows to be his little time, the time he tells me that he knows to be…measured out over lunch as he sat waiting for me to finish my *café au lait*. And the check, we found when we asked

for it, had already been paid. Beating in their many towers, Kirchberg's endless bells

chime. "They have lived here," he says of our hosts, with a shudder, "all of their lives."

❖

*Safer to stay in the*
*Out of which anything might emerge*

❖

You have put your finger on it, he said, or

That is exactly my point, in a tone of great sorrow,

Slowly shaking his head from side to side—

As if to clear it or remove some restraint—

There is no one of us whom we can trust to be objective in this matter,

Who does not have, that is, how shall I call it,

Interest in the outcome of this case.

(Or was it "a bet on the side"?) I hardly dared

To cry out, for fear I should say the wrong name.

"This house," he muttered harshly,

From between parched lips, "has been built on a grave."

*A night like any other*, his audience chimed in in something like

Astonishment,—what a sense of continuity you must have had!

He nodded quickly and brushed away with a rough hand

What might have been

A tear. And then stood up

    (All at once his audience vanished)

(As if in a dream)

As though to break

Something

      (You could not, from one moment

               To the next, be sure)

Fragile

    Into sharp-edged

        Pieces of

           "Where was I?"

(And what charm had brought me there?)


❖


"But she exists in pieces, if she exists at all, this woman," he had insisted, frantically. And so we were roped into searching for the clues. "I must build her up," he added, "out of these fragments." (It was, perhaps, *out of these almost non-existent....*) "Yes, yes," we said, "there, there, of course." "She exists as a whole," he finally muttered, "in my mind, only, and I must create her," he looked down at the dismembered, the tortured remains of, and then, despairingly, at his empty hands, "out of these." I think it is safe to say that he had, in this instance, our *complete* sympathy: so what if it was only 'a shallow grave'?


*(We were neither surprised nor unduly dismayed when she, "sobbing at times...said she could not recall some incidents she had once described in detail. After months of going over it again and again, she said, 'It becomes clouded.'" It was all getting cloudy....)*

The sudden slam of a door (but there wasn't

A breath of wind:

There was no one

In that room) and that music

Beginning again

*In the darkness*

In which he had sat down, so long ago, to play me

"A little composition of [his] own,"

*Un instant* the sound

Of breaking glass will shatter

Forever leaving

The countless tiny, curved, gleaming, dangerous

Reflections of instead.

❖

*(Then there was, if you will, a lull in the storm*
*[Of the personal].)*

# (A Word of Explanation)

"Something…something chased me all the way here!"

Were we getting to it at last, I wondered, the secret of the house?

He barged out of the study, flinging the door to behind him,

"Can't you shut her up?! These noises disturb me in my work." The Doctor…

I murmured. "The repeated," he sneered, removing his gloves carefully,

"And may I add expensive visits of your admired Silence appear to have done

Nothing for her." It's true, I admitted, I'm just a bundle of nerves.

We must find someone completely trustworthy to stay with her tonight.

He examined each of us in turn. I followed his gaze around the room.

It was then that I fully understood the horrid falseness of my position.

Wait—there is something I must tell you. "If it isn't already too late."

But if you expect me to believe you—on the strength of a *feeling* merely….

(It's just that the flowers you send, she said, seem to fade so quickly in this room.)

"I'm afraid I've had, old boy, a bit too much of your excellent vintage,—

Why, I seem to be finding a pleasing cadence in the most accidental of sounds."

Without silence, he added significantly, without the most perfect silence

I cannot continue. I could tell—I believe that we all knew as one—that horrible,

Even unspeakable experiments had gone on in that room. I refuse to believe

It is the fault of my dead wife. We could not get her to tell us what she'd seen.

"But if that's all it is," he laughed easily…. It was not, of course, all there was.

"Someone," he said, slowly, "who knows nothing of what has gone on here."

He looked at each of us in turn, "Someone whom we can trust to be completely

Objective." He rested his eyes for a moment on me. "Someone who will not be swayed

By any personal considerations." Wait, I said, there is something I must tell you,

Something I feel you should know. But it was too late, the walls gave way and I woke

To find myself in a room I thought at first I recognized. But I was wrong:

There had been some quite subtle but very significant changes made. I said, Wait,

Wait—this is wrong, this is all wrong. *Yes of course*, she said, *there, there.*

❖

In the lamplight, at dusk, in that peaceful room—whose windows were open to the sounds of summer insects (although a fire glowed on the hearth, reflecting back the lurid reds of the blown roses leaning in, and shining on the burnished leather and gilt bindings of the ancient tomes), in that quiet room—I knelt and examined my bloody hands, or "lifted these encarmined…" to my face. *In dismay*. A strain of what might have been romantic music, but muted, "as if from a distance," as though it were always already a memory trace. Of course there was some explanation. Satin cushions. The scent of dried flowers. The delicate web of cuts scored deep into the skin gave the impression of some fine and unusual lace. Something that might have been dirt under my nails. Perhaps I had had to dig my way out? Because that would explain a lot of things.

❖

He clasped his hands in front of him: the Doctor.
What had seemed to be merely a brief hiatus—
"I can't go on." That voice which,
Coming as it did on the heels of our despair,
Each one of us had welcomed as our own. "He seemed,"
Witnesses were able to assert much later,
"To have been speaking for us all."
To be in the grip, that is, of a much vaster sorrow
Than had hitherto been suspected. Surely it was no longer
(Blank) which was bothering him? "Cheer up, Blinky," one of his former

Messmates chided him, but the presence of this *souvenir*

Of less troubled times (of 'far less

Troubled times') only seemed to add another layer to his gloom.

Was it the silence which made us see

How the fire was sinking, how the curtains

Swayed though there wasn't a breath of air in the room,

How a hand reached up, apparently disconnected,

A fragment itself, to fragment

A glass against the wall or insist on

A whole that wasn't there, that perhaps had never....

Was it "a girl like any other," after all? Or

"A boy like..."? *It is,*

He was overheard to remark (you can find, still,

Survivors willing to stake their lives again on this version),

*The oldest story.* Or 'the oddest story'? At this point

His lips were hardly moving, his eyelids barely stirred.


❖


"I'd like you to notice," the Doctor broke off mid-sentence to warn us, "how certain themes, or, if you prefer, 'motifs,' seem to—in what we might otherwise find to be not even a series but merely a succession of apparently random noises—seem to," he repeated, "repeat themselves." "But it's strange," she murmured vaguely, glancing into the mirror, "that no one is there...for I had had, just now, the distinct impression...." "That someone was there," I finished, a note of what might have been triumph or sorrow creeping into my voice, "that someone was there you could trust, you could—even so briefly— lean on...." Did I say that, or had I merely broken into the seemingly endless laughter that sounded so strained and false to my own ears? Had I leaned towards her and, sinking my fingers deep into the shimmering blond waves, pulled those heavily rouged lips down onto mine? "It is not that simple," the Doctor reminded us, from behind those spectacles which had suddenly appeared, "there are certain aspects of this case which still require a word of explanation." We shook our heads, eyes shut, hands over our ears. He would insist, to the bitter end, that it was *a love story*. Someone in the back made a noise of polite disbelief. I peered in through the bars.

(There was, from the other room, the distinct sound of something Breaking.)

"Never mind," he shrugged, "never mind." It's been like that for days now, I whispered. *Like what?* he snarled, abruptly dropping his pose. He leaned closer and spoke in what was now a confidential tone of voice, "Can't you stop them?" I don't see how. He peered down at me from behind the thick lenses, "you are not" (and was it regret I heard in his voice, or impatience, or envy?) "exactly dying, you know." But he did not say that this condition could be cured. His audience confessed, as a body, later, to a certain disturbing sense of *déjà vu* or *je ne sais quoi*. It was the usual effect of this treatment. Another crash was heard, this time accompanied, sotto voce, by a volley of oaths. "It seems to be drawing nearer all right." A sudden hush fell upon the gathering. I kept the connecting door within my sights, not breathing. *Change*, he suggested, *the subject*. Was it at that moment that I began to suspect or had my first glimmerings about the possible significance of that oh-so-apparently innocent scrap of song? "You seem to have lost the thread of your narrative." *Pull here*, I read.

*"This face,*
*Eyes shut, and a bare shoulder*
*The edge of the sheet slipped away from*
*In that dawn*
*Light, in that light*
*The color of dawn...."*

❖

The ringing startled me out of sleep—the persistent ringing—and then a woman's voice (from beyond the grave). I lifted the coffin and listened, the smooth black receiver cradled in my trembling hand. She pinned the phone between her tilted head and lifted shoulder and lit a cigarette, sitting on the edge of the bed. I had to imagine her: flare of the match in a dark room. "I want you, I dream of you." Uh huh. Blow it out then. What *were* those noises, meaning what made them, meaning what motive and so on. Whispers. If you were the lover lying beside her the voice on the other end would sound like an insect (intermittent buzzing, out of which a pattern...), *would* be, for all you know, but we mustn't let our imaginations run away with us, *n'est-ce pas?* "I am," she spoke clearly, on this end you could clearly hear her say, "surrounded by ghosts." *Surrounded.* He lifted his pen from the paper (it ceased, the sound of that delicate buzzing scratch, ceased abruptly) and gazed at her for a long moment before speaking, before breaking the silence, no, no, before he turned to the window and, looking out, let what seemed to be a long silence 'fall' between them.

❖

*There was a series of high-pitched screams.*

❖

FICTION DEPARTMENT
Book Notes
DAMSELS IN DISTRESS

BLOODROSE HOUSE        1985                                  Cecily Crowe
New York divorcée Lucia Vail goes to the English village of Yorkshire to complete research for a biography of Charlotte Brontë. In England she leases Bloodrose House, named for the brilliant flowers covering the cottage. The villagers are intrigued by her and are pleased to have someone finally living in the long-vacant house. Lucia soon suspects her friendly neighbors are keeping secrets about Bloodrose House and its former mistress, the late Mrs. Helen Farr.

FLIGHT OF THE ARCHANGEL        1985                        Isabelle Holland
Kit Maitland's assignment to write an article about a Hudson River estate sale turns into a murder investigation, with Kit as the suspect. Additional complications occur when two men, Joris, her charming half-brother, and Simon, Kit's estranged husband, demand her loyalty. Her life depends on making the right choice.

THE GIRL ON THE BEACH        1987                          Velda Johnston
New Yorker Kate Killigrew goes to a small North Carolina island to seek solace after her break-up with her fiancé. She is fascinated by Martin Donnerly, a man she meets on the beach. Later Kate learns he has spent twelve years in jail for killing his unfaithful wife. Believing Martin is innocent, Kate decides to unmask the real killer.

DREAM OF ORCHIDS        1985                               Phyllis Whitney
The death of Laurel York's stepmother precipitates a chilly reunion with her estranged father and her two stepsisters. Laurel's stepmother died in the family greenhouse, where exquisite orchids are grown. Laurel's discovery of the secret of the orchids puts her life in danger.

❖

"There were two people in a room," —one of them might have begun this way, the long, difficult saying, setting the glass down— "two people in a room and though they spoke to each other they could not understand what the words meant, because they did not— finally—believe in either the existence of the person who spoke to them or their own. They felt, in a word, like ghosts haunting a world of things the reality of which they could only, with effort and briefly, intrude. 'Language built us,' one of them might have been confessing, sadly, 'Language could tear us down,' and the other would be sobbing, 'But there was no one in that room....'"

❖

The satin cushions. The bloodstains. The open window. And a sort of theme emerging, *too-ra-loo.*

# Pastoral Interlude

Our patient sleeping at last, I have come out into the garden bringing this novel with me: I do not think they will think of looking for me here, and I shall be able, perhaps, in these stolen moments, to get down, on the copyright page or the blank flyleaf or crushed in the margins, my impressions of recent events and order my all-too-scattered thoughts. It is crucial I think clearly, I know that, now more than ever, and yet my mind will stray...; how tall these walls of green are! How vividly each leaf in the hedge stands out, each gemmed with its single drop of water in this dense fog (O, the English summer!), in which I might be miles away from the house, so thoroughly is it obscured. I am sure they will not find me for hours; that is, I am *almost* sure...and this comparative peace and safety...but how can I expect you to understand how precious this time is: you, who are so far away from all that has occurred (you will find me much changed upon your return). The fog muffles their voices—I fear they have noticed my absence already—and somewhere close by in this blankness footsteps hesitate for an instant as though uncertain and then go quickly on. I don't dare even a sigh of relief, lest they hear me (and I have no need, of course, to vent *si vrai* a feeling in so theatrical a way); I must think clearly: I must get down, as objectively as possible, the horror of the past few days...I no longer expect you to believe me (I feel I have given up—or do I flatter myself?—entirely that hope which had once been, I confess it, *everything*), but I must, if for my own sake...it will be a kind of record after all, a weak, flawed record (written crosswise over the other text), yes, in this woman's handwriting—cramped and shaky—you must certainly despise, and yet there are parts of what I am going to tell you which may (and how my heart leaps at this thought!) be useful to you—and so, then, true...or do I mean true and then...? If I am not careful everything will, in this fog, fade and blur. Already the outlines waver; I must hold onto something (I must take refuge in description, I must convince you—before it's too late!—of my power to *observe*): the grey stone bench I sit upon, carved in its back, "Waiting," the single word; the bench which draws up from the earth its damp chill; the inscribed seat of dove-grey stone, yellowed along its scrollwork by lichens and beribboned at its base by those glittering traces of their passage the snails scrawl. There. I feel as though I could go on now, I can and must go on. It was last night, you see, at dinner, in that house, yes, *In that house whose baleful influence even here, even now…*but I cannot, must not give into these fears, these—you would say—fantasies…for you I must be lucid and strong; I must say, I must write, that is, without trembling, without allowing the trembling of my hand in this handwriting to show, simply, "It was last night, in that house, at dinner, my duties over…." It is much harder than I feared. (And there are footsteps, nearer.) I need time to get this down. There are waves of despair and doubt: you can't know; I'm sure you will never believe me; I don't think it possible, now, that you can return in time…; these words will never reach anyone, or—if they reach you (too late of course)—will not, by then, mean anything. They will not mean anything: they will fail to awaken any emotion beyond…; they will be as silent as I am, out in the garden (the formal garden, the heart of the maze), silent and still, only my eyes darting to follow the sound of those steps and the repeated low, sharp whistling—as though the keen edge of something (but what?) were being brought swiftly down through the air…and then the sound of this pen moving over the paper, sound I must pray no one hears…. I swear the events I am going to recount are not the product of my, as you'd say, overheated imagination: all of this actually happened even if some of it is not strictly, by your standards, true. I know how you appreciate these distinctions and so I make them. Each leaf with its drop of water, et cetera, the crunch of gravel, the soft whistle a long, pointed blade might make if it were swept repeatedly through the unresisting air. I must not let my facility with language (what you once called my...) run away with me (carry me away). I must stick to the facts. I must speak distinctly (clearly and with a certain volume, chest lifted, head thrown back) and to the point on those subjects for which I am qualified, my personal experience of which has undoubtedly qualified me to address: *Falling Down Through a (Hidden) Hole in the (Apparently Solid) Floor; Going Out in a Rainstorm at Night to Explore a Strange Noise in Thin Attire and with Only a Guttering Candle; Empty Rooms: How Empty Are They, Really?* (some examples from literature); *Dying*—or would it be *Kinds of* (ingenious, extraordinarily gruesome and noisy) *Death*—this last is rather suggestive...have I lost you? I must speak clearly, I must keep a certain distance, a certain objectivity.... I am afraid you will not even want to hear.... The whiteness of my hand on this white end-page; the blank wall of salty mist masking the house, as though someone had draped a huge sheet...—for what hideous birth, or bad joke about ghosts, or private examination?—...but no, I must stay away from the edges of metaphor (the deceptive edges of), I know that: it is the province of...'"the deranged',", yes, I think you'd insist on that phrasing. You see how I expect you? But I won't give in to these feelings of longing my efforts at perspective so thinly disguise. It is now some distance from dinner last night: years, years (you might think, by now, forgiveness was possible...you who weren't there, you who don't know…), and the food we sat down to then—that feast of anticipations—has rotted with the bodies of the diners whose graves we decorate ("the joke died on his lips," as we like to say, yes, *all* the jokes have…); and surely I can think of it objectively, from here? We were at dinner, it was after the fish course had been thoroughly applauded: dull eyes goggled up from the tarnished face that finished off the cage of bone. In the silence which fell we heard the next course announced (the bell-like tones of those who waited on us still ringing in the air) and yet I would like to insist that we did not hear, really, or that we failed to comprehend what we heard; we were unprepared; our imaginations failed us…. I feel you doubting me as I write these words: I do not believe I can ever bring you to grasp the extent of our innocence, yes, even in the midst (or perhaps because?) of the atrocities which then…—but I insist on this: we had no idea, we could never have imagined it. And yet some one of us had been able to, that was really the…horror: that another human mind, heart, soul (I want very badly to say *esprit* here, but I'm afraid you'd only read in that the effect of that costly and "worthless" finishing school you delighted in paying for), *had* been able to imagine it, which surely meant that we too, sooner or later…. (I want to postpone that moment as long as possible.) Surely I need not be more explicit? Surely you have already seen it all (or enough, at least, to allow me to leave that *all* there, suspended—a rare specimen, discolored and long dead, of some almost-extinct, et cetera—in your suspension of disbelief)? Who could assert with any degree of assurance that the house was still there behind this fog which so completely veils it now, behind this breathing wall of white (which distracts, which urges forgetfulness), or do I mean to ask, *Who could convince us now?* Everything fades, blurs; what isn't, as you once said to me, describing yourself, "hollowed out"? We were at dinner, we witnessed something, had to admit to the existence of something, have been forced to accept the fact of something we should have remained in ignorance of, we would have preferred to remain forever in ignorance of. Do you understand? Each leaf tipped with its single, tear-like (but no, not simile either) drop of water (I must hold onto this); the intricate turning, circle within circle (the going-back-over) which makes up the empty shell of a snail; the millions of sharp-edged, flashing fragments of proof we call the ground and walk on unthinking, which is not the same as "unconsciously." At least I know I am not dreaming—so grateful to have found this moment of comparative safety in which to write you—the details are too clear, too singular; the time too brief. I am sorry to be so good at this task you hardly dared to entrust me with; I know that, if anything, it is this which keeps me from being what I had so longed to be: believed. And yet I feel as though I had had to relinquish that thin hope so long ago I shouldn't even be able to recall having entertained it. What should I recall? The sound of footsteps approaching now, firmly (have I reached the end of my usefulness?), and the sibilant whisper, not of my name but of metal on air; that keen blade which does not find anything solid, which does not not find anything, that is to say, which resists it—you can see it all clearly now, can't you? Can't you? Someone *is* cutting this "fog so thick you could cut it with a knife," with a knife. Now the uncut pages trapped below your thumb become the dumb evidence, damp warped: *no need to read any deeper....*

# "A Pretty Girl Is Like a Melody"

What might have been wind slamming the door shut. But No no no, you don't seem to understand, (fastening up the metal jaws of his capacious black satchel), this fantasy version he has created of you, this, if you will, *doppelgänger*, or double—whichever you prefer—which he has perfected in (need I remind you) your absence, no longer depends for its 'life' on your existence at all. Indeed, it might be best to admit at once that this intricate machinery (and here his open palm began its slow crawling towards me, the motion of some hard-shelled insect caught on its back, legs waving, accompanied by a distinctly audible rachet-like noise, a ticking, as of some ancient clockworks) works, he went on, much better without you. What was it that stranded him there, repeating tonelessly— hand out in that timeless gesture—*without you…without you…without you…?*

❖

"I long for you."
Oh yes,—that one:
*I long for you.*

"Yer rroses 'er suhrly coomin' along bonny *this* yeer, ma'm."
He tipped his hat. "What? Oh, yes…"—distractedly;
Looking out on what seemed to be a sea of blood.

(IL TUE SA FEMME…—
In the *nice-matin*: the story about a man
Who killed his wife—A COUPS DE ROULEAU DE MACHINE A ÉCRIRE:
"*Il y a une mer du sang.…*")

Which lapped in sullen waves against what shore....

This shore (my adored)—
See: sea-shore,—everything infected by
That metaphor....

(Against which broke—in the *Times* and the *Voice*—
*"Blood, used needles, sewage..."*:
That long hot summer.)

❖

Squeezed out from these moments of time a few pieces of proof that someone existed: "suddenly the stairs..."; "I do not think she will be able to tell us what she's seen." A pause, "ever." Was there anyone who, on the bridge, had had the time to see clearly how the catastrophe—the impossibility of which had been so widely advertised—would in fact occur? Obdurate heart of what white unyielding...—why do you stay so far away? I sit here and spin these stories about you (and then undo them, of course), this thin web of lace I no sooner display the emptiness of than shred, pulling it quickly back out on the ebb. And after all these ominous. These ominous.

These ominous rumors of.

❖

She comes running up out of the darkness and past us, screaming. There is the sound of a woman screaming and then we see her, running down the sidewalk towards us and then through us; in between us (as though we who saw her, who cannot forget her—I know that you, as I, can never forget her—were not there) and then past us, and away. She is wearing a white blouse and a short black skirt and carrying something, what? I didn't notice, or don't remember. It was late: after midnight; a street in Northern California in 1976, in what was probably early spring, still cold. We stopped when we first heard the screams and just stood there, "like statues," slightly apart from one another, and she brushed swiftly through us as though we were invisible, as though it did not matter that we were there (if we were there for her): we couldn't help her. It was clear we couldn't help her (or I need to believe that?); it was too late and whatever was behind her, (there was nothing behind her, no one following her as she ran), it was much too late: there was nothing anyone could do (and what good do I expect this to do, now, showing how well I remember?): dark hair, her mouth open, on her face the streetlight gleaming, the shine of tears. Even then we thought we made her up: out of our own distress, out of the unhappiness which filled us and about which we couldn't speak; we thought we made her up, we needed her so badly, we needed her there and so desperately needed her not to be real: for whatever had happened to her, broken loose upon and in her, to stay far away from us; to be no one's fault; not to have happened at all. We didn't believe she existed, we didn't want to believe she existed. We wanted her even then to be kept like this—

something else we would never admit the existence of: she was the last piece of proof we needed, the final clue, the last lost scrap of evidence the witnesses keep, to themselves. Because to speak of it (This Really Happened?) might have made it less true? She was a special double-edged gift the night had given us, we thought; she was a test we had failed. She was a young woman running down a well-traveled street in the middle of the night screaming out of some pain we could not speak to or touch, This Actually Occurred, who flashed between us, through us, her face wet with tears and distorted, in her hands something…maybe her shoes? I think she may have been barefoot, or in her stockings —there was no sound of heels on concrete, as she came down heavily—and she was running, but her shuddering indrawn breaths were not for that, but because she was screaming, screams without words in them, just screaming, loud enough to hear from a distance as she came toward us, and in the distance, as she went away again, until the darkness and the silence took her back *as though she had never been.…*

# THINGS LOOK BETTER IN THE MORNING

We were at breakfast—and yet I could not but be struck by the wide difference between this gathering and that happier one of the day before. A whole world of innocence, or so it seemed to me now, had been lost to us since then. Oh, yes, certainly the light streamed in as before (through straggling clouds, and through the high and narrow windows of what some of us, at least, were coming to think of as our prison), touching to gem the jam, to glint back off the jasper surface of sausage and the pink marbled slab of the ham, where we sat, *as though carved out of stone....*

*No.*

We were at breakfast—but oh, what worlds, what chasms of difference lay between this gathering and that happier one of the day before! No one of us had remained untouched by this latest disaster. Horror was writ large on every face. "I hardly like the look of this," someone was heard to mutter, as we lifted to our lips those cups whose white surfaces were all but lost beneath grey drifts of what might have been merely ash but seemed suspiciously to function as a kind of fingerprinting dust. The sunlight faded in the staff photographer's repeated flash. The maid dished out what we understood to be the evidence amid a host of furtive glances. Indeed there lay such a web—constantly broken and repaired—of shifting looks across that laden board, as might convince the most impartial of our communal guilt and mutual distrust. A web all quite suddenly ripped to shreds as, with a twitch of lace, a flounce, the understudy made a bid for ingenue: "I cannot bear this one more instant!" (Notes in her diary later *The poisoned atmosphere; hysterical laugh-ter cut off by a turn in the stairs....*) We imagine her tearing at the windows in the safety of her room for "the sweet, fresh air"; flinging her valise upon the bed,—a force of nature! But the man she was to marry came to pieces under the Inspector's pointed ques-tioning.

*No. Not that either. Try once more.*

We were at breakfast, or we were gathered around the breakfast table, our eyes raised pi-ously to the weak sunlight which, filtered through the dirty glass and straggling clouds, turned to fire the open jar of marmalade: an opal jelly in which the opaque lines of skin swam. Narrow windows through which we, as they say, "took in" the scene. The Inspec-tor's forced good humor, "Here now, what's this all about!" Which seemed to strike, for what followed, if you will, the note.

❖

The floor solid oak (apparently solid); the walls lost under layers of mouldering wallpa-pers, tapestries, the endless dark tarpits, whoops, portraits the good family bones oozed pallidly up to the oily surface of (each in its ornate fence of chipped gilt); the high ceil-ings chased with a pattern in plaster, intricately worked but—white on white—difficult, from this distance, to really.... "It's an illustration, of course," he smiled grimly, "of a rather well-known story… a love story…," and he paused there, looking down through his empty glass to the waning fire, "but a story of such fragility I cannot be altogether certain that it will hold up in the telling." We leaned forward as if to assure him of our trust in his care. "My very touch, my lightest touch among these tenuous threads, may destroy it completely, and forever…as though I had lifted too roughly a shred of ancient paper, thin as a butterfly's wing." We gazed at each other in consternation; wasn't this exactly what we had always suspected: that the long night which pressed its sludge-black against the tall windows was the result, precisely, of our desire to see? "It is perhaps one of those things," he sighed, "which melt away to nothing under the pressure of our longing to be certain of its truth…." Impossible to convince you of the sudden sense I had of an almost palpable menace infecting the air, although exactly who or what 'lay under' this deadly suspicion wasn't at all clear. "An that's 'ow they works hit ma'm, beggin' yer parrdun," — first they come to investigate (what he actually said could have been "inveigle," or "invigorate"), and then there's murder done. I tossed him a few coins and jerked open the door, anxious, I confess it, to escape the stench of that poverty. "'The scent of that smoke-darkened…' wouldn't you say?" "Yes, Doctor." He seemed, all at once, profoundly affected, grasping his brow in one hand as though the weight of it were suddenly…— "this is *very* interesting." How could I know I had touched with my clumsy fingers the chords of a terrible melody and the source of his one recurring dream? "The what?" "The burning…." *Absolute piffle*, she cried, turning away with a flourish of lace to go back to her room, back up to her lonely room at the top of the stairs. "I would like you to meet my…"—but words failed me there. "There!"—directing my gaze with a hand that trembled—"it is impossible that you should not see!" "The impossible," I remarked, with a shrug, as I reached for the glasses and felt, in vain, for the ice pick, "is getting easier and easier to believe." He accused me of not caring: "You don't care," he said, "I…oh, dammit," fanning brusquely at that glowing miasma which threatened to assume a vaguely human form, "I do think we're beginning to *get* somewhere." But an inexplicable and horrifying turn of events interrupted the cure. But a…interrupted the cure. Interrupted the. Exultant laughter, fading slowly away.

# (Muted Sobbing Behind a Shut Door)

I need to construct a scene here, I can feel it, in fact I feel—as you may or may not have noticed—an increasing need to find some solid basis in sensuous detail at least if not in what are known as hard facts. So the sound, now, of my footsteps in the corridor; the smell—steaming up from the tray I balanced carefully, on which the fine porcelain and silver rattled—of a blood pudding; the increasing disturbance behind that barred entrance I made my reflective halt before: those terrible retching sobs. *This is going to kill you.* What? *The attempt to prove it really happened, is going to kill you, to finish you off, to do you in.* How long did it take me to realize I was no longer alone? He lifted the cover off the dish and closed his eyes above the dark mass, "as if she needed this!" And then laughed (stewed heart, boiled tongue), "can't you see how impossibly real she's grown?" Too close for comfort that heartbroken weeping improved in volume and tone.

❖

*The Narrator: a line of pale lash on paler cheek, her hands in what appeared to be gloves of white lace; a day off? "Can't you remember anything at all?" A ghostly face at one of the windows in what we had come to think of as the empty... ("But why would they keep," we wondered, "that section of the house locked up?"); a sobbing behind a shut door, or—still trembling, unable to tell us—having drinks forced down that terror-constricted throat, to clear.... She lifts from the tray one of the silver lids her reflected face slips down over, distorted and blurred. "They look," someone laughed—halting her gesture mid-air—"like Prussian helmets, don't they?" (Don't they?) And then helped himself generously to that still-warm.... A tear in the fabric of the story? "I'm drawing a blank again." We might have imagined that we had imagined the whole thing, but for precisely this…incoherence: gaps in the evidence which become themselves evidence….*

*Or:*

*The Narrator: setting his glasses aside and massaging his brow, a 'mechanical gesture,' rust almost invisible on his well-cut suit of black wool—clearing his throat—'of another era.' In the warm light that gleams along the shelves of leather-bound books behind him; in the light glittering among the curves of ornate gilt titles (illegible); shining back from his high pale brow and the dark silk of his tie; in the light that glints back suddenly from his discreet gold ring and pools, finally, in the glass full of amber liquid he lifts to his mouth with a hand that might well be shaking (it's hard, from here, to say)…a Vermeer? And "the birds and insects, in the green-leaved trees and long grasses of summer," he leaned forward, eyes shut… "an opera by Verdi?" His seemingly fluent French yet marked by the odd hiatus, "The language of…diplomacy." And the rust-colored stain deep in that monogrammed cuff? By his own admission, a "compulsive liar"—the only thing we could really be sure of.*

❖

Shock and fear made my hands clumsy as I fumbled with the heavy fastenings.

❖

"If we could only find our way back to those brilliantly lighted, splendidly furnished rooms." Of possibility? "No, no, no," flinging his hand out, "what could be, *après tout*, more possible than these?!" Indeed. And yet it sometimes seemed to me.... "But we appear to have failed," smiling into his fist, faking a cough, "to have held her...interest." And in fact the sound of that heartfelt sobbing rose from behind the locked door, gaining volume until it was easy to imagine her prone on the bed: the rough texture of the warm wet linen her swollen eyelids and half-open lips were pressed into, the give of the mattress under the shoulders which shook and the legs which lay as though weighted— "easy to imagine," but difficult to speak of (I had to be sure he understood about the locked door: that she was she, inside, and I was I, out here). *And yet I saw he could not repress, when my damp hand brushed his accidentally, an almost invisible shudder.* "We must be careful," he admonished, "that we do not indulge either her or ourselves too far in this particular fantasy...." Had I 'made up' that voice which added, Here, why don't you go cut some flowers? He would watch, I knew, from the window and dress me ("'in his mind's eye'") in all—the mass of embroidered brocade my drugged limbs dragged against, the muddy disorder of pearls and furs and silks and lace, the raw crude red of my mouth...—I seemed to him to lack, in the lovely morning, in the perfectly lovely morning, in the perfectly lovely wonderful marvelous....—I dug the blades savagely into the stems.

# THE PROOF

It's *mechanical*, he insisted, disgusted at having been taken, even so briefly, for such a fool: these powerful emotions (he drew this part out on that board the black of which had long ago disappeared below the dense web of white laid down by the wiles of Theory), "fear," for instance, or "love" (and his laughter rang out, sharply), can be said to provide a kind of glue in our minds which joins, which holds together these discrete features, these body parts and merely instinctive gestures, to make of them at last what can appear—at least for a time—to be a seamless whole, a *gestalt*, if you will, and so, he smiled, "seductive," or "frightening." Remove these emotions, however, he continued, and approach these phenomena as we must—dispassionately—and you will find yourself confronted by fragments, solely: affectless pieces to which the connections are, the coherence is, he snickered, *missing*. Trust me.

❖

How had she managed to get up there, I wondered, surprised to find her framed in that high window. I shut my eyes and tried to recreate her passage through the cobweb-choked hallways, the rat-infested, empty rooms whose smoke-darkened still lifes mouldered, where the abandoned furniture loomed up, pale, sheeted ghosts, or lay in pieces on the floor, buried in the torn papers, rotting books, dust. I imagined the marks she left in her hurry: the traces of pointed toe and stiletto heel, erasure of grime where a short, flounced skirt...; drift of a heavy French scent; how a dark smudge might look on one of those large, soft, full, white breasts. "Where have you been?" I murmured, tugging gently at the already low lace edge of her dress, leaning forward, lips parted for the taste of ash, cold dirt on that sweet warm flesh, her cloying scent my breath, this ghost come back…. I pulled harder and the rotten lace curtains ripped, came apart in my grasp; I hurriedly wrapped my hand in the shreds and bashed a fist out through the window— *fresh air*—if only it wasn't too late…. "You've wrecked the view, of course." I flinched at the sound of his voice but stayed where I was, mouth to the broken glass. "Here," he said, "you look like you could use a little of this." He held out a silvered flask on whose curved surface my white face, distorted, swam. "She stood still," he wheedled, "she trembled under your hands." The face at the attic window a fist in its nest of rags. The fragments of glass on the floor—was it my imagination?—rubied along each glittering edge. "There are things here," he said softly, "which we may never understand…."

❖

"Darling," I murmured, trying to shape again the words of comfort he had given me, but I had never so fully realized their poverty. "'An explanation…,' 'perhaps a human agency?' '…very, very far away…'"—I looked away, afraid he might guess I no longer believed. Somehow I managed to grasp the cold hand he flung out toward me, and we waited together in a silence I hoped would soon turn in my back that silver key. "Darling…darling…." Could it have been that I had only imagined, lit red by the dying fire, that lurid scene? Perhaps you made it up, I sneered inwardly, from some terrible personal need. With an effort I placed that rigid palm against my cheek. How could I have even wondered—wasn't so great a gap in the image he wished to present simply unthinkable? It could never, I repeated to myself, have been. But those other hands reflected back in the silver lid they lifted away, still—the palms inscribed with a web of deep cuts— bloody...? "And nothing," he might have said, but so low I could not be sure he had spoken, "will ever be clean." It was no use: I couldn't ask him to tell me the truth—he would turn away, *laughing hollowly,* there would be the sound of hollow laughter and the crash of something breaking no one threw. And I would only have a confused impression of what followed, later..."you were dreaming," he'd say. And yet the taste still on my lips of that sweet warm salty.... (I must have been *dreaming.*)

"Cut," I stammered, trying to read that awful writing, "to pieces."

Or was it in fact *to please?*

❖

"Objects come and go," he laughed (the faintly quizzical look, the lifted eyebrow, the characteristic half-sketched gesture of one of those fine long pale hands), "they just come and...go." "Yes, but not," I protested weakly, leaning forward to snatch my cup from the wobbling tray, "usually quite this quickly." "No, but I simply take this," seizing his tea and a last chunk of cake as the service rose into the air beside us, "with some gratitude, as a daily lesson—writ in a print admittedly somewhat larger than life—on the transitory nature of 'things.'" From somewhere behind us came the sound of porcelain smashing and the splash of cream and tea. "It *has*, of course, its awkward moments,—but what doesn't, really? And then too," attempting to hide a smile, "it does scare the women off." (The curtains billowed in suddenly over the tightly fastened windows, a muted strain of romantic music seeped in from beneath the shut doors and that vague blue glow in the hallway—I'll swear to this—threatened to assume a vaguely recognizable form.) "Oh well, but...." "No; you must admit I am no longer considered the 'catch' I might once have been." "But surely," I suggested, "you must have someone in...to clean?" "I try," and an all-but-imperceptible shudder shook his slender frame, "not to think of these things." (Had I stumbled, purely by accident, onto the gaping flaw in his philosophy?)

(I observed the widening hole with dismay.)

"The 'splash,' that is (for I had failed to take the precaution of glancing backward at the time—into the wreckage, *the end of an era*—to verify my facts and now, too late, as my ears grew sensitized to that uncannily steady drip-dripping, certain questions began to occur to me), of what I had assumed were 'cream and tea,' 'of what I had wished to assume,' or, 'of what I had been delighted to call, formerly....'"

(And so I kept, for awhile, my *sangfroid*, as it were: kept the full horror of our situation from bursting in upon me, involved, as I was, in the play of these nuances, these shadowy shades of meaning which whirled around me like leaves, like leaves....)

(The gaily colored corpses of which I awoke to find piled around me.)

❖

*Inscribed on the hand she lifted away from the serving tray's silvered lid, the intricate web or net of livid scars, white on white: a word? A signature?*

❖

"Humph, no," he said, stolidly, "doesn't sound like a good thing at all to me: teacups whizzing about the room and such." (It wasn't a teacup at all, you old boob, but a water glass. It missed his head by a mile, too—how could he object to that?) But these things, "these little things," call up, you know, the most unpleasant recollections. "Ah yes," a dreamy, nostalgic look on his face, "It was the beginning of summer, the insects chirring in the tall grass…." "'And the dry rock no sound of water,'" I filled in hurriedly. "Yes," he said, "you know this part?" "Lie down," I said, "I know this part." "'And the cricket no relief,'" we continued together. "I could swear," he said, sitting up abruptly, brow furrowed, "that these seemingly random noises kept hesitating on the verge of becoming a recognizable tune." "'It *is*,' said the Doctor, 'a fashionable grocery list.'" Which seemed to say pretty much all there was to be said about that.

# THE ILLUSION

*"But nothing is what it seems," he murmured at last, sighting along the length of his umbrella,*

*"and perhaps it is simply true that we are all, finally, most present to each other in our absences:*

*that we have to leave, as it were, in order to ever really arrive...."*

❖

Of course I'll be all right here Darling, run along now. But I had to prove it to him—but

you had to prove it to him, didn't you: to let him hear the screaming, to show him the

bloodstains, "like roses"—were those the words that escaped from those dry, still lips?

What an apt pupil. To get him to scent, as you did now, frequently, the intermittent

stench of some putrid decay on the air. Not at all like roses. I could hardly believe my

ears. But you must trust your senses. It says that? Yes. Disbelievingly, you mean you just

sat there, the tea things whizzing about your head, trying to deal reasonably with that

spectre? "Yes, yes," irritably, a motion of the hand as though to wave away, belatedly, those

memories, or was it merely that annoying cloud of—but what was it and where had it

come from?—vague blue (in which I almost recognized, in which I almost thought I

saw...), or was he merely setting out, one hand at a time, into the great gulf misunder-

standing had opened up between us?

❖

*We must make certain that all of the windows are shut.*
*Yes. The curtains closed and the doors*
*Locked. Yes, yes, a chorus*

*Of voices chimed in dutifully.*
*Is everyone in agreement that there is no other*
*Method of egress? Yes (but this said*
*With less certainty). Then turn the lights off.*
Now *(the voice disembodied, gloating),*
Now we shall see.

❖

But what reason, I mused idly, as I watched my husband draw back from the perforations he had made, could any of us have for not wanting to *know*—much less standing in the way of the evidence (Darling, he asked wearily, for what must've been the hundredth time, *could* you, please…just a little to one side?)? Or standing, I added privately, in the way of a clear view of the lack of same. But "There are crucial gaps in your account of this affair, missing pieces in your story!" He flung down pen and paper impatiently (I'd like to, I confess it, see him raving or roving now between his empty chair and that long window, never glancing backwards at that so disappointing a dreamer on the couch: striding up and down, 'like a caged animal,' as though he could feel and could no longer bear the quotation marks and parentheses which so closely surround…). "She would tell us if we coaxed her," he wheedled, "she would tell us if we charmed her," he cajoled. Wasn't he longing to ooze through that locked door and bring his precious sensitivity to her like some kind of obscene present? I can't imagine anyone who less needs, I sneered, your facility with guilt and sorrow! As if on cue—and well out in a clearing so that their shine would be caught by the starlight—he "burst into tears." Or, "he dissolved into…" (well, all right then, *began quietly crying,*—if it means that much to you).

❖

"A consummate 'woman's book.' It offers escapes to castles in Austria, to villas in the south of France,…to Hollywood and even further to films being shot on location…"
—*The Washington Times Magazine*

"It is easy to want every item [(blank)] catalogues, easy to imagine wearing it, eating and drinking it, driving it, smelling like it.…" —*Los Angeles Times*

"She gives the reader a close look at a real English castle, where priceless armor, paintings and antiques embellish room after room…[this book] is about emotions and feelings and I found myself moved." —*Los Angeles Herald Examiner*

"Meant to be read in a peignoir on a chaise lounge whilst daintily nibbling scented chocolates." —*Cosmopolitan*

"The surprise ending is both poignant and fitting. It is also a reminder that the past is never really over." —*San Diego Union*

❖

*To break the glass and then force her to crawl through it, roll in it, as in "roll over and play dead"—perhaps he had (perhaps I had) imagined that. Someone had imagined it. The Ingres-like expanse of smooth luscious white flesh being cut, opening up: the small red mouths appearing as if by magic all over her body (the glass transparent, as in "not interfering with this purely visual pleasure"), like stigmata, saying* please. *"As if by magic," because there is no sound of screaming, there is no record of the screaming which might have been there (her mouth is open), there is no soundtrack to this movie (not interfering). Why are your hands so cold, why are you shaking? That's all it is, après tout, a harmless…fantasy. He turned to me in the dark and smiled, harmlessly. A bad dream, that's all. You must have been dreaming.*

❖

With one hand I waved the crowd of closely pressed onlookers back, "you 'saw'," I repeated, as gently as possible, the few coherent words she had gotten out—"you 'thought'?" But she shook her head, she shut her eyes, she wouldn't look at the glass we held up to her mouth. "Nothing," she whispered, finally. "'Nothing'?" I repeated in disbelief. She shot me an accusing glance. I swear I started out only pretending not to understand but, after awhile, I really didn't. What would a language fragmented by fear look like, anyway, I wanted to ask. But it was much too late, of course, to undo all the work of those long years of what we were told was merely *politeness*.…

❖

"Not," he smiled ruefully, shaking his head, "that it's a very good illustration of the story. There are scenes, even crucial scenes," lifting his almost empty glass up into the light, "left out.…" He swirled the slivers of ice and the dregs of his potent drink around and looked up. "But it isn't a story with which I would like to leave you," he lowered his voice and gave the heavily veiled windows a self-consciously 'significant' glance, "on a night like this." Why didn't we tear those curtains down there and then, and confront him? Force him to look at the greying sky, grab him, and shake him, grind into those increasingly blurry features the sharp intelligence that there never had been "'a night like this,'" break the glass; why did we sit there, letting his eyes cloyingly linger on each one of us in turn, winding that sticky trail of weak goodwill around the room as he gloated *pianissimo* over what he was pleased to call the new "stability," the new "permanence...."

❖

## COMME MARILYN JUSQU'A LA MORT
**La vraie mort...**
**... de la fausse Marilyn**

Le sosie de Marilyn Monroe, un mannequin britannique, a été retrouvé mort dans des circonstances qui rappellent la mort de l'actrice américaine il y a vingt-sept ans.

Un locataire a retrouvé Kay Kent, 24 ans, nue et allongée sur son lit....

On a retrouvé près d'elle des tablettes de somnifères et une bouteille de vodka à moitié vide. Des photos de Marilyn Monroe étaient éparpillées sur le lit. La pièce était également remplie de livres et d'interviews de l'actrice enregistrées sur des cassettes.

Kay Kent a seulement laissé un message a l'intention d'un amour d'enfance...qui commence ainsi: "Cher..., je t'aime tant."

Les parents de l'admiratrice de Marilyn ont précisé que les ratures rendaient le reste du message illisible.

### Morbid mimétisme

Kay Kent tirait la plupart de ses revenus, 60 000 livres annuels (environ 612 000 F), d'annonces publicitaires pour la télévision, les restaurants et les magasins où elle incarnait la star d'Hollywood. Sa silhouette était bien connue des Britanniques qui avaient coutume de la voir dans la presse populaire.

Elle avait perdu sa mère il y a trois mois et venait de rompre avec son ami....

*"Elle vivait tellement pleinement son personnage de sosie qu'elle ne pouvait pas s'empêcher de mourir comme son idol"*, a déclaré son frère....

Marilyn Monroe avait été découverte morte dans son bungalow près d'Hollywood en 1962, avec auprès d'elle une bouteille vide et des somnifères.

❖

*"It's a dream," he said, "it's only a dream. There are forces beyond our control. There is a good explanation. There are reasons for every single one of these sounds. (It is only a dream.) There are things here," he added, "which we may never understand."*

# THE EMPTY ROOM

In between: those vast spaces we preferred to think of as empty. "Do you have any idea," this out of nowhere, irritably, "just what you mean by that?" He doubted (and who among us would have claimed he was the only one?) I could live up to his fantasies. "You have to take into account"—or was it, more clearly, 'pack extra clothing for'?—"the person he imagines you to be." And indeed I was, as that little voice had suggested, 'haunted,' by what I thought of as this potential—running my fingers through the thin fabrics—for *love* and *happiness*. I imagined all those visions which had darkened our hopes and dreams had fled completely: that this sunny morning had restored to us, in some exemplary fashion, our equally sunny trust in one another, that its innocence, in short, was bound to be ours…but it seemed all was not as it seemed. "Do you have any idea what you're doing?" (As though he could see me through that paper!) No-dear-what-dear? Pulling the roses up one by one from the vase set in the center of the break-fast table and tearing the petals savagely from their stems…so that the white cloth was spattered with a sudden rain of dark red. Oh-dear-I'm-sorry-I-just-wasn't-thinking. Never mind. Just then the maid came in with the brains: came in much worse for those experiences at which we could hardly begin to guess, but somehow knew 'must have been horrible,' with the brains. *Isn't there something you'd like to tell us; isn't there something you feel we should know; aren't there any words you're longing to give us we can take with us into the darkness into which we must every one of us sooner or later go?* It was difficult, even 'terribly difficult,' watching from this distance, over all the intervening, which had conspired to render these events ever more…. I forget what we said then, looking into those flames into which the last and only solid piece of evidence had been consigned. Was it in fact that fire whose ashes we would sift so hungrily, later, This Really Happened, and hold up in grey handfuls as *proof* and *the only basis from which to decide...*? (That and the ominous lifting of music from a farther room, a room we would swear was empty.) (But for the broken shards of...curved, reflective, glittering dangerously.) "These memories," he attempted, beginning again, only to be cut off by that voice full of 'fascination and horror,' *A love story*? So you say. He begged us, then, to let him off the tale he found himself in such severe danger of marring, "through," or so he would have had us think, "sheer fatigue,"—promising that he could take up these tangled threads at this same point tomorrow, and that nothing would be (by a brief hiatus, "a mere instant, really, of inattention,") lost or transformed; but that the truth might be, in his words, lured closer, by our so pointedly looking away.... But he was unable, at that juncture, to convince us, and indeed—as he confessed much later—they would have been, no doubt, subtly altered by that bath of shadows he so longed to dip them in: "they," these thin and even, one might go so far as to call them, flimsy characters.

❖

*One Last Letter*

6/22/88

—

I am surprised that you consider silence an effective form of communication; you are, after all a poet. I wish you would have let me know sooner as I just sent another note the same day I received your card. Thank you for responding though, better late than never.

Just for your information, I didn't assume anything…but rather, my purpose was to be romantic and playful. I apologize if I frightened or offended you in any way. Don't worry about your privacy, I won't even talk to you if I see you in the street. One other thing I would like you to know is that I am a realist, have been around the block many times, and am a serious and shy person…I do respect your feelings and desire for privacy, so since we'll never see each other again I truly wish for you the best life ever.

Sincerely….

❖

"These depressing moments…" (he trailed off; I took up the trail where he left off); *When you lose track of whatever it was you were following in the traces of.* "But that is not it, exactly: I have not lost the scent of the game but the heart for the chase: for this waiting to recognize a pattern in these apparently random, these unconnected…, for the clues to fall into place, for the evidence to mount (like a sudden fever, that hectic flush) and take on, all at once, an irrefutable form and structure. Do you understand?" he asked, but as if in spite of himself, "it is, I dare say, tragic, but that instant for which I had lived, formerly—in which there would be no gaps in the argument, in which it would be 'air-tight,' so to speak—" (I looked with new eyes at the mess he had made of the windows) "is an instant in the existence of which I can no longer believe." What had changed, I pressed him, rifling through the case histories to which, now, I could hope to add nothing (and which, in turn, had been hopelessly tainted by his disbelief). Is it, I mused aloud, that there is a flaw in one of the highly complex theories with which we began this experiment? It is nothing, he sobbed, but errors from beginning to end. And yet it was crucial, he added, turning towards me slowly from his rather, I thought, exaggerated "business" with the door, crucial that we get both the diagnosis (what *we*, I asked, but alas much later) and the specifics of the medication right this time. He put a hand he must have meant to be soothing somewhere. "No, no—don't go in there…there isn't a chance he'll know you" (or was it 'a prayer'?) "as a being whose life is actually separate from that of his imagination, but I cannot, of course, answer for the consequences—to you both— should he come to doubt this…and we can never," he continued sternly, "be sure." *Well then what am I paying you for?!* But I was, quite naturally, "in your debt for whatever sum you should mention…": the black bag snapping shut with some finality; as though in just that—the shutting door; the narrowing mouth of the satchel in which the wink of blue steel…; the spotless fingers curling over the cash I laid to rest in his palm—lay the cure. (Lay what we had come to think of as….)

❖

But things did *not*, in fact, look better in the morning, rather, the pitiless light put a harsher glare on it all: the forks and knives left there as though dropped from a height, abruptly; the gleaming shards of what might once have been a glass; the rubied glop— on the shining white linen—of something that might have been strawberry jam. But "finish your meal," or "Don't mind me, go right on eating"? It was too late now, far too late, to ever turn things back to whatever pretence at normality we might once have enjoyed. She stirred faintly, and her eyes fluttered open, meeting mine. "What…, what happened?" I glanced back over my shoulder quickly but the Doctor shook his head with a frown. "Nothing," I said, "just one of those little lapses." "It could happen," another voice chimed in (too eagerly?), "to anyone." "But how did I get here?" she asked, pushing herself up weakly from the improvised bed we'd made her. "Hush, hush, there now—don't try to move just yet." I made a pillow of my arms and she sank back into them, gratefully. *There is somebody here*, I remembered the Doctor's words, vividly, *in whose interest it is that she never remember....* Did he know what seeds of doubt he'd planted then, in my fertile imagination: that I would never, could never, be sure it hadn't been...? "We were at breakfast," she murmured sleepily, "yes, it's all coming back to me now." (Was it all coming back to her? She must have felt my arms tighten around her neck; she must have seen my fixed stare....) "'The pitiless light,' et cetera,"—she half-opened one eye and then shut it again. "And then?" Someone from the back asked breathlessly, and the cry was taken up, "And then, and then?" I knew at once how distressing it must have been for her: to have come back to life in what was clearly the middle of the night; that *dark and stormy* and so forth crushed juicily up against the bare windows, a crowd of pitying faces pressed closely around, and a few discordant notes from a distant piano the only response to the Doctor's repeated request that "the lady" be given some 'air'. "Who are you," she breathed, with what was, at last, in her voice, the beginning of real terror, "and where am I?" It was then, I think, that we felt quite sorely the absence of the one person who might have been able to tell her: who would have been able, that is, to account (as someone would have to, sooner or later) for all of those missing hours, those lost years....

❖

"It is not a story," he confessed, finally (or so I read by the weak, trembling light which fell on the yellowed page…), "with which I would feel comfortable leaving anyone I cared for alone—to feel its coils drawing close around them, and closer still, and then finally to feel themselves unable to speak of the awful significance just now becoming all-too-certain: beginning, that is, in the tightening grip of that logic, to…*choke*…."*

❖

Who was he talking to, anyway? He waved his hands in the air, he gestured wildly. The wind blew, the gold sunlight, filtered through clouds, gleamed dully on the ice. What was he saying, what was he trying to say? The charred timbers leaning at crazy angles cast weird shadows in the weak sunlight. There was the stench of burnt wet paper and the singed edge of a leather spine caught my eye; light glinted in what was left of the gilded lettering…. We must have been standing in what once was the library. Above all this the scent of her perfume, sweet to the point of revulsion, bitterly sweet, still clung to the air. His coat the white of the snow, which, slipping down from the broken roof and through the shattered floors below, was lying in drifts around us. "I'm freezing here," I said to

---

*As if to illustrate these words his blackened tongue protruded from his empurpled face and his rolling eyes bulged, horribly, while his arms' crazy windmilling sent his empty glass to shatter against the wall. The infamous 'dull thud' alerted us — eyes fixed on those ice cubes a little less distinct each second in the long puddle of golden liquid — to the apparently inevitable consequences of trying to make anything that clear.

him, "aren't you?" His face the same absence of color, his hands as well, and from his dry lips anxiously working, no sound. "How can you bear it?" I asked him. The wind tugging at what was left of the curtains. "I'm fine," he said. The expressionist sketch those blackened broken windows were, against all that white, I wish I could tell you, the roughest outline of what might once have been a door....

I had to face the fact that I was alone:
Completely alone in what could only be described
As the wreckage of my former life. "Unless you can recall these rooms,"
I said to myself, "exactly as they were—
Richly furnished and full of warmth and light—
You will not be able to escape this waking nightmare."
As though all that kept me from crossing those vast, empty, echoing
Spaces was a lack of the proper nostalgia:
My inability to come up with a convincing,
If somewhat soft-focus, frame and....

The squeaking hinges of a door pushed carefully open; the pounding, steady and slow as a heart, up the stairs; the note that read *I never meant to hurt you*, the fragment of ancient, yellowing paper, the barely discernible words....

# THE CURE

I slammed shut the door of the empty room and walked back down the hallway to the kitchen, and standing at the sink, I said, "Well, that's that," as lightly as I could. "What's what?" the apparently solid wall of newsprint asked me, "I mean," my husband cleared his throat, "what is?" "She's left us." "Just like that?" His pale face seemed to rise above the crumpled *nice-matin* like a disbelieving moon (on whose surface I might have seen my recent enlightenment reflected). "Just like that," I echoed, "without a single word of explanation." "And she would have needed," he said, but as if to himself, "a lot more than one of those. Well, I'll be damned," raising his voice to be heard above the sound of running water, "left the evidence, I imagine for us to dispose of, hmm?" "On the contrary," slipping the soap in as an excuse for this wringing of hands, "there isn't the slightest trace of her. Indeed," I went on, "we might have an exceedingly hard time convincing anyone that she ever existed…anywhere, that is, outside of our minds." "A shared hallucination?!" he scoffed. "Let us say rather, a metaphor…." "Paugh!" I could read the mingled disgust and relief on his face as he turned his attention back to those other, more speakable disasters. Glowing in the uncapped jar of marmalade, in the melting butter, the shreds of orange pulp caught at the rim of a glass, the scraps of egg: the morning light gave the littered table a festive air. "We shall have," he muttered finally, "to advertise…." But his voice trailed away to nothing and I found myself looking blankly back at him in a terrible hush in which the steady dripping of the hands I held out (*too late*) formed the only sound. I don't think it had occurred to me until that instant to wonder if anything else besides 'the proof' were missing: whether, that is, we had merely exchanged that fragile silence of hers for a measurably more obdurate one of our own.

❖

"She touches me and takes her hand away abruptly…."

It's so clear that there is no one, that there never was anyone

There. *These candles,* I heard myself apologizing softly,—

And the curtains swayed inward suddenly, though there wasn't a breath of air.

These notes from a farther room, an empty room; the sound

Of glass breaking and then silence, heavy…bitter.  Each of us, he said,

In this family, has been stalked by a singular doom. There was a dull thud

As the Doctor let fall the hand he had lifted between his own.

What was the emotion I felt, I wondered, as the flames licked through the structure

I had called my *box of dreams*; as the walls dramatically caved in…?

Was it mere relief, the "Ay an yer weel out 'o thar sur," as Bill so plainly put it?

(Tip him!) I doubted my feelings were that clear…wasn't I, after all,

Already better able to remember it than when I had been free to 'check' my

impressions:

Wandering—notebook out, pen lifted—from room to vanished room? Wasn't I

not-so-secretly

Grateful to have come to the end of that frightful inventory: to be able to group it all,

Now, under a single word and a wave of the hand, *Gone…?*

Already I felt nostalgia blooming within me: its obscenely soft pliable petals

Unfolding one by one: the stench of fog rising, of fog and wet burnt wood;

Mold and dust lying thick on the rotting fabrics; the curtains torn down,

The windows shattered; and the dank earth, the decaying vegetation;

And the wind which lifted faintly to my ears the foghorn's keening knell.

I would nourish this flower, regret, I promised myself, then, silently—

Hadn't I been willing to give up everything I loved to give it room to grow?

*These candles,* I tried to explain, but quite unnecessarily now.

❖

Were those tears? Too late I had begun to wonder—that wet substance: that glittering mess on the floor by the wall; that steady dripping…, had it never been a tune at all but something abstract (behind it) like Sorrow? Was there really something here all this had 'stood for'? Was it too late to be asking these questions, as I feared? To be asking questions and to sometimes, I confess it, have been actually making assertions in the query's thin guise,—these strange markings, where had they come from and what could they possibly mean (and was it true, as the Doctor assured me, that the answer to the former question would go far towards answering the latter as well?)? Too late, of course, I realized there was something I had to know. And so I rushed out in the middle of the night, the storm, the flimsy stuff of my gown, *Uh huh*, the pitch darkness, *Yes*, briefly lit up by the glare of the lightning, as though a gigantic flashbulb…, *Are you sure, my dear*, he said, removing his glasses, *that these images are your own* (or 'that these words are…')?…no answer, sigh, *Go on*; the pouring rain and my gown clinging closely to the curve of thigh and breast as I fled, *Yes, good* (reassured), with only this one small candle, *Ahem* (I look over and see him penciling in a question mark in the margin by "small"), in the direction of the graveyard…; *Ah yes, now we're getting somewhere, aren't we, yes I think you're well on your way to what we might call a complete cure, although, of course, we never use those words: definitions, you know, heh heh, not very easy things to fit real people—with all their little frailties and foibles—into, but I think it's safe to say that you've come very far and surprisingly quickly* (self-conscious 'eye contact', 'hearty' smile), *and I* (his professed distrust of the self, of course, only serving to give the confession more weight), *I've enjoyed, heh heh,*

*working with you... but I'm afraid* (acting out "brightly cheerful in the face of adversity" —

for me to imitate?) *we've come to the end of our time...* (afraid I'd misunderstood him?), *our*

*hour, I mean, for today....*


Or was it blood...?


"Blood?!" "What, did I...yes?" Exaggerated patience and something else (what?) lurking

just underneath: "you mentioned blood, darling." "Did I?" Brow furrowed, a look of

distress, the now-why-on-earth-would-I-ever-have...; 'a foolish thing like...'—glad to find,

under the arrangement of roses, the dead dark red bits of... scattered across the white

linen when, "so silly of me!" Sweeping it out of sight and mind with a gesture that maybe

too much resembled an arm outflung for the safety of rock, beach; the apparent shore of

resemblance: simile. Ah yes but of course and the understanding smile, the silence that

heals as the wall of words (This morning's headline: GARE DE L'HORREUR (("Que

s'est-il passé exactement? Personne ne peut le préciser...."))) goes up between us again.

"Darling?" "What now?" "Nothing." How mention, how make a place on the seemingly

smooth surface of this self-consciously bright and sunny new beginning for the sound of

that steady dripping, the all-but-unrecognizable rhythms of which do not cease (in what

we do not cease to regard as the background) their ominous beginnings.

❖

He was right: it would kill me to make her real, to believe in her, I could see that now. To go on breathing, in order for me to go on breathing I would have to repeat (after him), *her lips of ice, her breasts of snow.* "How white she is," we would murmur in unison, "how white she is and how cold." "And if you held her"—this was my difficult solo—"if you ever tried to hold her…she would melt." "My clothes would be ruined," he grinned, "my face would be covered with tears." How could I have dreamed a mark on that white skin, of a cut deep into that skin, and of blood, of color and warmth and odor? "Call her 'Blanche,'" he laughed, "or 'Bianca,' see how perfectly white and cold and unmarked she is, she always was. Call her 'Claire,'" he smiled, shrugged, "I honestly can't remember…."

❖

*"It is a story," he began again, "it is a story…." But he choked; the words died in his throat, the marks on his throat, he cleared his throat—"I'm sure every one of you knows" (or was it "could supply"?) "the ending of…."*

❖

"I don't think," he said, one ear still cocked to the 'natural' mayhem outside (to which his mind had, so briefly, given an order), "I'd better have another one."

"I think I'll just take these dreams," he said, smiling down on her, "up to bed where they belong."

"This is where I draw the line," he laughed, "this is where I quit: when it all," he flung a hand out loosely to the green of lawn and bough this late in the spring, this early in the summer, "when it all," and here his laughter became a little shrill, "becomes a little song."

❖

How to let go, how to just walk out, the sound of your footsteps tacking the To Let sign back up in the cracked window, your sigh of relief serving to rearrange the cobwebs exactly as they were before you came. Does the dust lie back down in a smooth blue mantle? Do you walk backwards out of the room, the house, the town, protesting—at last— an innocence no one ever doubted; "I never touched anything"? Is it really that 'no, not a single backwards glance' time? (Time to take it on trust, time to leave it behind...?) Had things ever been been any, well, let me know if things had ever been any different (or is it 'seemed'): *write to me.* We'll never know what it was now, will we? A considering glance up at what used to be the attic: a ragged line of debris against the clear sky, "If it was anything." "No, no," closing the car door firmly or snapping to the wide-mouthed satchel, or pressing the hat that shadowed his face down more securely, his eyes narrowed, "I suppose we never will," a pause, "not now." Our eyes met. Cash changed hands. "'And so we turned our faces away from the scene of our doom...'"—the cars drove off in opposite directions.... Dare I admit that, behind those dark glasses, I turned my eyes back for a last long look at that smear of red (the late roses, of course) festering in the front garden, the gate we had shut even now swinging open, the door we had locked already agape too? It was then, I think, that I resolved to say nothing of what I had seen: to have...a secret, yes; an unlighted area all of my own, an apparently empty room (boarded up, barred, no access, no entry, forgotten, nearly, no trespassing): something, some place, that is, within me but not 'mine' at all (to say, to sign away, to sell),—wasn't it, I breathed at last, un-speakable? Had I spoken aloud? "At last," my husband laughed, but in a voice I no longer recognized, "we are alone!" I hardly heard him, busy saying over to myself the words *words fail.*

❖

And came to slowly, *"I don't,"*
One hand held up against the glare,
*"Remember."* Anything?
What looks exchanged
Above that slumped, white-shrouded
Shape already blurring
At the edges, losing
Definition even as we watched?
*"There were these..."*—
One hand outflung, a gesture, empty—
And then? *"And then
Nothing."*